She was staring at him, eyes wide and amazed, and he couldn't believe it, but he could feel it. Heat, a goddamn wall of heat pressing in against him that hadn't been there a moment ago. His lungs suddenly felt soupy, and his eyes burned with it, as if he'd opened the door to a blast furnace.

Charlie twisted her hand up to clutch his wrist, hanging on. He stared at her, sweating already, amazed that this was real, actually happening just the way she'd described it. That she had been through it before, all alone, and hadn't freaked out, hadn't run screaming from the house, hadn't simply passed out from the sheer intensity of the temperature shimmering the air around them. Even the candle blazed brighter, feeding on it.

The chill bleakness of December, a chill that had clung to this room, utterly vanished.

Her fingers tightened and he dropped his eyes to watch, feeling the sharp bite of her nails in his wrist, and then realized why she was doing it. There was more. More than just the heat. Under its surface, a ripple, a vibration, was something else.

BOOK YOUR PLACE ON OUR WEBSITE AND MAKE THE READING CONNECTION!

We've created a customized website just for our very special readers, where you can get the inside scoop on everything that's going on with Zebra, Pinnacle and Kensington books.

When you come online, you'll have the exciting opportunity to:

- View covers of upcoming books
- Read sample chapters
- Learn about our future publishing schedule (listed by publication month *and author*)
- Find out when your favorite authors will be visiting a city near you
- Search for and order backlist books from our online catalog
- Check out author bios and background information
- Send e-mail to your favorite authors
- Meet the Kensington staff online
- Join us in weekly chats with authors, readers and other guests
- Get writing guidelines
- AND MUCH MORE!

**Visit our website at
http://www.kensingtonbooks.com**

Christmas Spirit

Amy Garvey

ZEBRA BOOKS
Kensington Publishing Corp.
http://www.kensingtonbooks.com

ZEBRA BOOKS are published by

Kensington Publishing Corp.
119 West 40th Street
New York, NY 10018

All Kensington titles, imprints, and distributed lines are available at special quantity discounts for bulk purchases for sales promotion, premiums, fund-raising, educational, or institutional use.

Special book excerpts or customized printings can also be created to fit specific needs. For details, write or phone the office of the Kensington Special Sales Manager: Attn. Special Sales Department. Kensington Publishing Corp., 119 West 40th Street, New York, NY 10018. Phone: 1-800-221-2647.

Zebra and the Z logo Reg. U.S. Pat. & TM Off.

ISBN-13: 978-1-4201-0819-4
ISBN-10: 1-4201-0819-0

First Printing: October 2009

10 9 8 7 6 5 4 3 2 1

Printed in the United States of America

Chapter One

Interview me, baby. Now. It was all Charlotte could think when she saw him. For some reason, she'd expected a reporter out of a 1940s movie—rolled up shirtsleeves, wrinkled tie, a fedora, a notebook. What she got, she thought when she opened her front door and faced the man standing on the front porch, was something else entirely.

"Sam Landry," the man said, sticking out his hand with something less than a friendly smile. Something closer to a scowl, in fact. "With *Scoop*." He flashed a laminated ID badge at her, and she was pretty sure she wasn't imagining the distaste in his eyes.

Well, he definitely hadn't stepped out of an old movie, Charlie thought as she put her hand in his. He was twenty-first century all the way, faded jeans slung low on his narrow hips, a dark blue, long-sleeved T-shirt untucked above it, a parka with a fur-trimmed hood, and at least a day's worth of stubble above his lip and along his jaw.

His wide-set blue eyes narrowed when she simply stared at him.

God, he was . . . gorgeous.

"Charlotte Prescott?"

She swallowed hard and shook his hand absently as she found her voice. "Yes, that's me. Charlie. I mean, you can call me Charlie. Short for Charlotte. Everyone does."

He lifted an eyebrow, dark sandy brown like his hair, which spiked up in the front as if he'd run his fingers through it. It was sort of mesmerizing, really, how nice his hair was, even all ruffled that way.

"So . . . can I come in?" he asked finally.

Heat flared in her cheeks. *Snap out of it, Charlie.* "Of course," she said quickly, stepping back and waving an arm toward the gloom of the entrance hall. "I'm sorry, I'm just . . ."

Well, there was no way to finish that sentence without embarrassing herself, was there? What was she going to say? *I'm just surprised because I watch too many old movies and you are so not old? I'm just incredibly nervous that a guy who looks like you is going to interview me? I have no idea how to flirt but I want to?* She was uncomfortably aware of the wire-framed glasses perched on her nose and the fact that she hadn't done anything with her hair but leave it to hang against her shoulders, as usual.

She smiled weakly and closed the heavy door behind him when he stepped over the threshold, catching a faint whiff of something male and spicy, like a ghost of scent behind him.

A ghost. Right. That was why he was here, not to steam up the parlor she was going to have to redecorate as soon as humanly possible after Christmas had come and gone. Hooray for the holidays. She had a reason to hang lights and glittery things to distract visitors, not that she had many, from the not-very-successful mix of delicate antique chairs and a brutally modern sofa.

"Have a seat," she said as brightly as she could manage, taking his parka when he shrugged it off and gesturing to the most comfortable chair in the room, which was soft and wide and covered with a grandmotherly chintz. He would make a nice contrast, what with all that rampant virility he radiated so effortlessly. "Would you like something to drink before we get started?"

Those deep blue eyes were blank and bored. "I'm good, thanks."

She sat up straighter, smoothing her hands over her knees. Well. He wasn't very nice, was he? He wasn't even prepared, she noticed, as he flipped through—finally—a small black notebook and took out a pen before he laid a mini tape recorder on the coffee table. He looked like he'd just rolled out of bed, in fact, and here it was noon. She'd been up since seven and writing since eight, curled up with her laptop in the room she'd turned into an office upstairs, with just her coffee and Butch for company.

Which was exactly what she'd dreamed about

when she inherited this house, she reminded herself when an unexpected pang of wistfulness hit her. Just because this guy looked like his to-do list included dangerous undercover reporting about drug cartels or mobsters, or maybe jumping out of airplanes and going behind enemy lines, didn't mean that holing up for a year to finish a novel wasn't a perfectly valid goal.

She was trying to decide if she was irritated with him or with herself when he looked up with a smile that was trying for charm and not quite succeeding.

"I'm new to the magazine," he said, sitting back, ridiculously huge and male against the flowered cushions of the chair. "I didn't actually have much time to look at the information before I headed out, so I want to verify a few basics before we start."

She suppressed a frown. Forty minutes on the ferry from Falmouth to Martha's Vineyard should have given him plenty of time to review his assignment—even longer if he'd come from Hyannis—but she wasn't going to be picky. She was still surprised that he had called in the first place.

"Sure," she said simply, sitting back and pushing her glasses back up her nose while he wasn't watching.

"So, you're Charlotte—I'm sorry, Charlie—Prescott, and you just moved into the house?" He glanced up from a page of notes scrawled in a small, almost illegible hand.

"That's me."

"And the house was"—he consulted his notebook again, and she wondered if she'd imagined the contemptuous tilt of his eyebrow—"inherited?"

She couldn't quite stop a frown this time. "Yes, it's been in the Prescott family since it was built. My aunt died earlier this year and she left the place to me." She paused when she caught the expression on his face, boredom now mixed with unmistakable contempt.

And she had no idea what that was about, but she felt herself bristling the way Butch did the first day they'd felt the ghost. Wasn't a reporter supposed to be impartial, or at the very least interested? It would be nice if this one was polite.

But no.

"So you inherited this big old place and you're planning to live here year round now." The statement—it definitely wasn't a question—caught her by surprise before she could come up with anything to say about his attitude, and if she'd doubted it even a little bit before, there was no mistaking his feelings about her now.

Misguided as they were, she thought darkly.

"I'm not sure this is a good idea," she said, hating the stiffness in her tone. "I mentioned the ghost to a friend here, the lady next door, and I really never imagined anyone would be interested but me. And you seem to be more interested in, well, I don't know what, but if you're implying I'm some kind of a spoiled heiress who's planning to stroll around Martha's Vineyard in

gem-encrusted high heels and . . . and go yachting
or something—"

"Whoa!" He held up a hand, a sheepish grin on
his face. "That's not what I was implying. Or
what I meant. Or maybe it was. I apologize. I
didn't get much sleep last night and I don't know
very much about ghosts or haunted houses or,
well, you. And like I said, I'm—"

"New to the magazine," she finished for him,
and tried to look away from his mouth, which
was wide and amused. He probably was a wonderful kisser, she realized, and felt her cheeks
flame again.

Okay, stop that. This was business. Of course,
since it was business, he had no right to flash that
grin, which was hot enough to warm up this bone-
chilling winter day. He shouldn't be allowed anywhere within a fifty-mile radius of a convent, for
sure. Goodness.

He sat back, one ankle resting on the opposite
knee, all lanky, lean confidence, and she fought
the impulse to take a good long look. Staring at a
point just beyond his left ear was probably safer,
she decided, and willed herself to stop blushing.
It was completely unfair that he could turn on
the charm just like flicking a switch, especially
when he'd as much as admitted he was being rude
earlier.

"So," he said easily, his tone amiable. "You've
inherited this house that you believe is . . .
haunted?"

"Yes, I do," she said, drawing herself up to her

full height—mentally, at least. The house was haunted, and she knew it as well as she knew her own face. There was no other explanation for the things she'd heard and seen and felt since moving into this rambling old place, which certainly dated back far enough to have a rich history.

He raised his eyebrows. "You want to tell me why?"

Yes, she did. She really, really did. And this guy with his doubtful grin and easy charm wasn't going to talk her out of it. With a tight smile, she stood up and nodded at the kitchen. "Why don't I make some coffee and explain it?"

Charlie Prescott had backbone, Sam had to give her that. He followed her down the wide front hall to the kitchen, squinting a little in the house's gloom. She looked as if a challenging glare would knock her over, much less a feather, but there was a spine beneath that plain gray sweater and a definite stubborn glow in her eyes.

He swallowed down the faint taste of guilt. Served him right, didn't it? He wasn't exactly exuding enthusiasm, much less manners. It wasn't her fault he was here, working a story he would have laughed at even way back in college, when writing anything and getting paid for it had seemed like a victory.

"Have a seat," she said, waving at the mammoth oak table in the middle of the kitchen. He blinked as he looked around the room, moving over to scrape a chair away from the table slowly. The few things that had been renovated here had to date back a while, he decided. The lemon yellow refrigerator looked like it had come straight from the early sixties. Hard to believe it still worked and *why do you care*? he asked himself silently. He hadn't come over for dinner or anything.

She hadn't gotten around to her Christmas decorating, if she planned to do any. He'd noticed some holiday cards—Santa, elves, poinsettias— when he came in, left around to sparkle sadly as if she'd forgotten about them.

Most of the rest of the kitchen reminded him of stepping into another century entirely. The few cabinets were old wood, painted dozens of times. The floors were wide-plank, worn with age, maybe even original, and there was a tall hutch against one wall filled with floral china. If he blinked and blocked out the refrigerator he could imagine candles burning during an evening meal, a woodstove over in the corner beside the hearth.

"I have some modern conveniences," Charlie said, and he glanced up to find her smiling nervously at him and pointing to a shiny black coffee maker. "Don't worry."

"Hey, it's cool," he said and sat down, the wooden chair smooth and warm. "Hell, it certainly looks like a haunted house."

She arched an eyebrow at him and he threw up his hands in apology.

"It's a great old place, Charlie, but it is sort

of . . . well, old." Um. That didn't come out the way he planned.

As if it mattered, he reminded himself. He wasn't here to flatter her. He wouldn't be here at all, reporting some bogus story about ghosts, for God's sake, if he wasn't working for *Scoop,* the journalistic equivalent of a goddamned Twinkie.

And he was only working for the magazine temporarily, he reminded himself with a silent growl. Before too many ridiculous stories about celebrity comebacks and rock band feuds and haunted goddamned houses ran with his byline right there in black and white.

"The house dates back to the mid eighteen-eighties," she said simply, and pushed the button on the coffee maker before taking thick white mugs out of a cabinet. "But modern houses can just as easily be haunted, you know. It's not the age of the place, it's what happens in it."

"So what happened here?" he asked, setting his notebook and recorder on the table.

She shrugged and shook her hair back. It was golden brown, the color of sweet, dark tea, sort of pretty, really. Behind her glasses, her brown eyes were intelligent, the kind of eyes that noticed everything.

"I have no idea." She leaned against the counter and folded her arms over her chest. "But I do know what I hear and what I see."

He tilted his head, watching her as she crossed the kitchen to get milk out of the fridge. Absently, she took out a quart of eggnog first, then put it back and got the milk.

The thing was he didn't doubt her. She sounded perfectly serious, and perfectly sane, to boot. He wasn't sure if that was crazy or frightening. Ghosts didn't exist. Come on.

Of course, there was no way to judge until she actually gave him the details. "What do you see?" he prodded.

She blushed a little then, faint color on cheeks that were completely free of makeup as far as he could tell.

"I'll admit I haven't seen the ghost as much as I've heard it," she told him, still pink. The coffee bubbled in the pot and she dragged the mugs closer to pour it, dark and rich even from where Sam sat. "And I've . . . well, I've felt it."

She shot a sidelong glance at him from under her lashes. Felt it, huh? He cleared his throat to disguise a bark of laughter and ran a hand over his face. This should be good.

He was definitely not making enough money to sit through this crap, even if Charlie was sort of infuriatingly adorable.

"I know it sounds crazy." Her tone was equal parts embarrassment and determination. "But it's true." She handed him a steaming mug and nudged the milk and the sugar bowl across the table.

He frowned when she left hers black and scalding. The coffee was strong enough to put a few more hairs on his chest, and he'd added a generous splash of two percent and two teaspoons of sugar. "What do you mean you feel the ghost?" he asked, trying not to scowl when she blew on her coffee delicately. She had a soft pink mouth with bow lips, and for a moment he could see exactly what she would look like if she were to kiss him.

Jesus. What the hell was wrong with him? Charlotte Prescott was about as far from his type as Alaska was from Brazil.

It was the job, he thought as he caught himself admiring the smooth slope of her cheek. If he had a real story to sink his teeth into, something to investigate that mattered, for God's sake, he wouldn't be so distracted, so restless.

So very appreciative of the gentle swell of her breasts under her thin gray sweater.

She didn't seem to notice him staring—she was focused on a point over his left shoulder, thoughtful, as a curl of steam swirled up from her mug.

"It's . . . heat," she said. "An intense, almost suffocating heat that makes it hard to breathe." When she finally looked at him, there wasn't a trace of guile in her eyes. "It's not quite something you can touch, more like a cloud or a haze, you know?"

He didn't, not by a long shot, but he nodded anyway. With a flick of his head at the mini recorder, he asked, "Can I turn this on?"

"Sure." Spine straight, eyes clear. She wasn't backing down.

He pressed the button carefully, slid the thing closer to her across the table. "Go on."

"I feel it most often in one of the bedrooms

upstairs," she continued. She was staring at the recorder a little suspiciously, but she went on. "Not the master bedroom, the smaller one in the northeast corner. The first time, I was in there exploring shortly after I moved in. It was late afternoon and I was simply poking around, taking the sheets off the furniture, admiring it all. Some of it is as old as the house."

"Taking the sheets off?" he said with a frown. "I'm a guy. Explain."

"You put sheets on furniture to protect things from dust. The room had been shut up for a while even before Aunt May died," Charlie explained with a sad little smile. "A few of the rooms were shut up, too, even when she was healthy. It's an enormous house for one person, and she was worried about the salt air and all that."

"Ah." He tried to look knowledgeable about the effects of salt air on fine old furniture and nodded. It was easy enough, if a little depressing, to imagine a woman living here alone, rattling around in the huge, gloomy rooms, only books and maybe TV for company in the off season and the long winter months.

Like Charlie would be, he realized. Despite the good fortune of inheriting a huge old house within spitting distance of the beach, right on Martha's Vineyard, she certainly wasn't flaunting it. She hadn't changed one thing in the house since moving in, as far as he could tell, and the car in the driveway was a sturdy little Honda with more than a few years on it. For some reason, he'd expected an eccentric rich chick with nothing to do but get her name in the papers, and Charlie was about as far from that as you could get.

He was slipping, he thought, resisting the impulse to run a hand over his face wearily. You didn't judge an interviewer going into it. You asked questions, you listened, you did the research, you told the story as objectively as you could. He'd learned that as early as college, when he wrote a piece about the evolution of gang warfare in Los Angeles.

Of course, facing weeks of research on the coastline's haunted houses, when he didn't for a minute believe in ghosts, was bound to make him a little cranky.

"Anyway," she went on with a wistful smile, "I was in there poking around one minute and the next I had to sit down. The heat just enveloped my entire body."

The heat must have enjoyed that, he thought irrationally. Something in her tone made him look up from the depths of his mug. Embarrassment? Unease? He couldn't tell, but she was blushing again, cheeks hot with color.

"There must be more to it than that," he said softly. Interested, despite himself. God, he really was losing his edge.

"There is." Her fingers tightened around her mug, knuckles going white with pressure, but she looked straight at him, eyes wide and unafraid. "And if you come upstairs with me, maybe I can show you."

Chapter Two

She should have known better, really, Charlie thought an hour later, sitting stiffly on the edge of the unmade bed in the spare room, Sam beside her, solid and male and patently disbelieving that anything was ever going to materialize. The truth was that she'd never felt that strange heat, sensed that awful, desperate need this early in the day, and she had no idea why she'd thought she could summon it at will.

Stubbornness, she supposed. It wasn't as if she couldn't read Sam's skepticism as easily as a giant headline, after all. HOT GHOST OR HOME-OWNER HOOEY? She could see the front page now, complete with a photo of Sam's smirk and a caption. *Our Reporter Gets the Scoop for Ya!*

He scratched his head idly, and she was pretty sure he was doing his best to hold back a yawn. Damn it. The ghost or spirit or whatever it was—she personally liked the word specter—was real, really, truly real. And now she was determined to prove it.

"It usually happens either late in the afternoon or at night," she said finally, hating the note of desperation in her voice. "And it usually surprises me. By the way, you might want to make a note of the fact that it seems to like eggnog, and it prefers the kind I make fresh."

Sam looked somewhat impressed. "I didn't know anyone made fresh eggnog. All I've ever had is that gooey stuff that you get at the supermarket."

"It's not difficult. I'll give you the recipe—real eggnog is actually like a protein shake but sweet. Anyway, I bought some of the readymade too just to keep him—her—it—happy. The ghost definitely spikes it. The level of the whiskey bottle keeps dropping." She hated the *uh-huh* look he gave her.

"I see," he said.

A master of tact, she thought wryly. He was probably thinking that she was hitting the whiskey, downing it in teacups, starting at breakfast.

"Eggnog. Fresh. I made a mental note," he said briskly. "Anything else?"

"I don't know where it comes from or why."

"No family history?" He stopped himself. "I sound like a doctor or something. But you know what I mean. Were there stories of it appearing to some people but not others, visitations at a certain time of year, anything like that?"

She shrugged, a motion that continued into

her raising her hands palms upward. "Dunno. Maybe . . . maybe it only appears at Christmas, like the clanking character with all the chains in Dickens."

She could not for the life of her think of the name of the spirit. Kick in, English degree, she commanded. Nothing doing. Sam Landry— being on the same bed as Sam—was a potent distraction.

"Marley. *A Christmas Carol*. Right."

She looked at him with a little surprise. Maybe he'd been an English major, too, doomed like her to a lifetime of scratching to make a living. Another reason to like him as much as she lusted after him.

"But it doesn't clank. Or maybe it knows we're waiting and it's . . . shy?"

The moment the word slipped out she wanted to kick herself. But when she saw the expression of weary incredulity in Sam's eyes, she decided she wanted to kick him.

"I'm really not crazy, you know." She stood up, stretching legs which had gone stiff after an hour of sitting immobile on the bed. She'd left the curtains drawn, keeping the light out, and with most of the furniture shrouded in sheets once more, the room certainly felt spooky, stripped of any personality or signs of life. "I'm not some New Age woo-woo type. I have a master's degree in American Literature and I taught high school English for seven years."

"What happened?"

"My last red pencil broke and I decided to quit. That was just before I came up here. But the point is, people trust me with their children and, yes, I am sane. I'd never even thought about ghosts before I moved in here, not outside of fiction, anyway, since the book I'm writing sort of hinges on the supernatural, but I know what I've seen and heard and felt. And this house is haunted."

She took a deep breath, surprised at herself. She sounded so . . . determined.

Sam, on the other hand, looked a little stunned. He blinked once, and then breathed out something like a laugh as he ran his hand through his tousled hair.

"You're writing a book?"

She frowned. "Yes, but that's not the point. The point is—"

"You think the house is haunted. Believe me, I get it." He grinned at her and stood up, and when his fingers curled around her wrist, she nearly jumped. His hands were huge, which wasn't a surprise since he had to be over six feet tall, towering over her barely five feet five inches, but his grip was also amazingly strong. And masculine. And warm. And wonderful.

Oh boy, it had been a long time since a man had touched her. And a man like Sam had never touched her, ever.

"We've been sitting here for an hour without talking and to be honest, I'm falling asleep," he said as he tugged her toward the bedroom door. "You know what they say about a watched pot."

"Yes, but . . ." She glanced over her shoulder at the dim, hulking shapes of the furniture, crouched there under sheets, and knew it was useless. There was nothing in the air, none of that strange crackling electricity she usually sensed.

"I have another appointment at three," he explained as they headed down the stairs.

Damn it. She should have told him more about the house's history, the day she'd heard the laughing voice in the upstairs hallway, all of it. Instead she'd made them sit there in silence, waiting, awkward, and bored.

Not that it mattered, she told herself as she followed him back into the kitchen. So the house wouldn't make it into yet another article about the haunted houses of New England. It wasn't even her idea, and part of her wondered if Aunt May and the rest of the family would be turning in their graves if they knew she not only believed in some kind of spirit life in the house but was telling people about it.

She'd moved in here for one reason, giving up her tiny Providence apartment and quitting her job—because Aunt May's death had given her a place to live rent-free and the modest money that had come with it was going to allow her to take a year off and finish the book she'd started back in college. She didn't have time to waste worrying about a cute reporter with a wolf's grin and an attitude the size of Canada. The article didn't matter.

But proving herself to Sam Landry in some small way did. Especially when she looked into those sharp blue eyes and saw herself reflected there, looking like some nerdy schoolgirl who lived with her nose in a book and had finally let her imagination run away with her.

Which wasn't too far from the truth, she realized with a pang of dismay.

"Why don't you come back?" she said suddenly, stepping in front of him when he'd gathered his things from the table and turned toward the hall. "Tonight. Sometime after dark, not too late." She sounded a bit desperate again, but she couldn't help it at the moment. "I've heard or seen things several times after dark, in that room. Really."

He studied her, and it was hard not to squirm under his gaze, wondering what he really saw when he looked at her, what he heard in her tone that she hadn't intended.

"How does eight sound?" he asked a moment later, with a gentler smile than she'd seen yet.

"Eight sounds perfect," she said, and let herself breathe again.

He nodded, eyes glowing. "It's a date, then."

Ulp.

"No, it's not," she rushed to protest, following him into the hall, heart pounding. "A date, that is. Um, I mean, that's not what I meant, I just wanted to give you a chance to—"

"It's just a figure of speech," he said, and the way he was very obviously trying not to smirk infuriated her. "We can call it a stakeout if you want."

She flushed. "Well, that's a little closer, yes."

One side of Sam's mouth curved into a smile then, sly and knowing. "See you at eight, then."

She stood staring at the door when he was gone, torn between frustration and excitement and enormous dread that they would spend another few hours sitting in silence while the ghost stubbornly stayed away and made her look like a fool.

Butch curled around her ankles, his tail flicking at her calf. He stopped and looked up at her, narrowed gold cat's eyes disdainful.

"Oh, what do you know?" she said out loud, and trudged back upstairs to her desk.

Two hours later Sam was fairly certain he should have stuck around at Charlie's, no-show ghost or not.

"Let me show you the videotape now," Marie Fogwell said, sorting through the mountain of books and papers on the roll top desk beneath the window. "It's a bit grainy, but you can clearly see the outline of Captain Grayson on the stairs . . ."

"I, uh." Sam stood up so suddenly, he actually made himself a little dizzy. If he sat here for one more minute listening to Marie ramble on and on about poor doomed Captain Grayson and the way he liked to hover near her shoulder when she was drinking her tea in the evenings, he would probably be certifiably insane. "I think you've told me so much already, and so . . . you know . . . vividly that a tape could only be a disappointment."

Marie hesitated, clearly hovering between pride

at her storytelling skills and disappointment that he had rejected her best prize, and Sam turned on his smile. "You've been so helpful, Mrs. Fogwell," he said, and crossed the room, notebook and recorder already stashed beneath one arm, to take her hand. "I'm eager to get back to my room and write your story, I hate to wait."

"Well . . ." Her pale wrinkled cheeks colored prettily and her faded brown eyes were shy as she looked up at him. "I can't wait to read it, of course. I keep a scrapbook of all of the stories about Captain Grayson, you see."

Of course she did. Along with the dozens of books about whaling, ships, Martha's Vineyard history, men's clothing in the 1800s, paranormal phenomena, haunted houses . . . He brightened his smile and withdrew his hand slowly. "Soon you'll have one more," he reassured her. "I'll let you know if I have any other questions, but for now I want to thank you for your time and sharing your story with me."

All said while backing slowly toward the front door, conscious of the overlapping braided rugs on the floor and the dusty knickknacks crowded up to the edge of every available surface. Good thing old Grayson couldn't knock anything over, he thought.

"Oh, of course, you call me anytime," Marie said, hand over her heart. "I'm always happy to discuss Captain Grayson."

Oh, he was definitely getting that idea, all right. He didn't breathe a sigh of relief until he was out the door and inside the Jeep he'd rented just yards away from the ferry dock. Tossing his notebook and recorder on the seat beside him, he leaned his head back against the seat and groaned.

This was only the beginning, too. He'd started here on the island, where the weather was bleakest, because he wanted to get it over with. No snow, nothing photogenic. The dunes seemed huddled down against raw, scouring winds off the ocean. What a time to come back to the Vineyard after all these years. And he had twelve stops to make when he was through here, up and down the coast from Maine to Connecticut, and would have to listen to a dozen wishful, starry-eyed, completely ridiculous stories about mournful spirits and cold spots and banging noises and otherworldly noises coming from the attic.

He gripped the steering wheel so hard his knuckles ached. He needed a drink. Or a convenient coma.

Six months ago he'd been researching an in-depth piece on poverty in America. Before that he'd tackled a U.S. senator's military record, which had turned out to be a lot spottier than he'd claimed, and before that a gritty, close-up look at hard drug use among teenagers in a small Illinois town.

Now? He was writing for *Scoop* and talking to sweet little old ladies who had clearly memorized *The Ghost and Mrs. Muir,* and a stubborn, shy, strangely kissable young woman who was probably having hallucinations.

His cell rang, rumbling out the first few bars of a Kelly Clarkson song. His last girlfriend had changed it the day they'd broken up, and he couldn't figure out for the life of him how to reset it. He figured it was probably a good thing he'd ended things when he had, or he might have found his laptop swimming in a bathtub full of water.

"This is Landry."

"Dude. Hey. Kev here. How's Martha's Vineyard treating you?"

Sam stifled a groan. The last person he wanted to talk to was Kevin "Hey-Dude" West, his new editor. He was barely out of college, wore colored contacts, and seemed convinced that being assistant features editor of a national entertainment magazine made him some kind of media mogul.

"I just got here, Kevin." He let the last word linger, and couldn't help smiling. He could practically hear the guy vibrating with irritation.

"Sweet. Just checking in, dude," Kevin said finally, voice as smooth as ever. Sam heard the background chatter of the busy New York office, a female voice laughing and a phone ringing. "How did the first two interviews go?"

Well, aside from the fact that he could have conducted them in his sleep after interviewing the heads of drug cartels and mob families, pretty well, he thought.

And since when did he need to be checked in on? He wasn't some novice reporter who didn't even know how to write a lead. He desperately needed this job, but he hated it, put it that way. But he had no right whatsoever to whine, he told himself. Newspapers and magazines were shutting up shop right and left and he read the AP and Reuters feeds—the whole country was wracked with economic woes. Get a freakin' grip, he told himself. But he still wasn't going to let Kevin be the boss.

"Kevin, I've got a lonely old belle in love with a ship's captain who died a hundred and fifty years ago, and a young woman who doesn't even know what she's seeing or hearing or whatever the hell it is she claims is happening. And for the record, I don't even know why *Scoop* is running this piece. It's not like it's going to be 'Haunted Houses of the Rich and Famous.'"

"Angel Pants, I said half-caf, not decaf, and extra foam, not none," Kevin said, not even bothering to cover the mouthpiece. "Sorry for the interruption, dude. I mean, it's just coffee. How hard can it be?"

For an assistant who let a jerk like Kevin call her Angel Pants and make her fetch him a foofy latte? Pretty hard, not to mention pretty goddamn stupid. He felt sorry for the girl.

"Anyway," Kevin went on, not waiting for Sam to answer. "We're branching into some travel pieces, trying them on for size. So the up-and-down the coast thing is, like, right. And dude, all that paranormal shit is hot right now. People dig being scared."

Sam was clutching his cell so hard, he was

going to crush it any minute. If this smartass kid called him "dude" one more time . . .

"I'm expecting an awesome piece from you, Landry," Kevin went on, obviously oblivious to the frustrated outrage that had to be blasting through the line. "I think we really connect, and there are a bunch of story ideas I want to dialogue with you when you come in."

Sam narrowly avoided banging his head on the steering wheel. Kevin mangled the English language like it was an empty soda can, and he was supposed to take him seriously? "I'll be in touch," he growled instead, and hung up, tossing his cell into the backseat.

Suddenly an evening with Charlie Prescott's shy smile and stubborn eyes sounded like the perfect thing to take his mind off the disaster his life had become.

Chapter Three

"Charlie? You home?" Lillian Bing pushed open the back door to the mudroom off the kitchen, Gloria's nails clicking on the floor as the dog preceded her into her neighbor's house. "Charlie? I brought day-olds from the store." She doffed her coat and hat and waited.

"Hey, Lillian." Charlie smiled as she walked into the kitchen, leaning down to scratch Gloria behind the ears. "I thought I heard a faint-but-familiar crackle."

"You did. One more time." Lillian set a white paper bag on the table and crackled it very loudly. "I got lemon squares, blondies, and two chocolate croissants. Gingerbread women, no men. And a nice fat shortbread Santa."

"I thought you said no men."

"I have absolutely nothing against men in the least," Lillian protested. "I wish there were a few single ones in my age range on this island but no. Anyway, I think of Santa as kind of sexless."

"Really? I wonder how Mrs. Claus would feel about that."

"After being married for a thousand years, probably grateful. Anyway, I know you enjoy treats, unlike the stupid carb-fearing masses. People will drink all the coffee in the world, but baked goods are apparently the devil's work."

Charlie grinned and peeked into the bag, giving the contents an appreciative look. "Well, they may be, but I'm willing to sin a little now and again."

Lillian laughed out loud and patted Charlie's shoulder. "That's my girl." She paused and tilted her head, considering the high color on Charlie's face. Leaning closer, she sniffed—her friend was wearing perfume, too, if she wasn't mistaken, which was unusual. In the two months Lillian had known Charlie, she'd never seen her in anything other than jeans and sweaters, the occasional plain cotton blouse. She didn't wear makeup, not that Lillian thought she needed it, but here she was in some kind of light floral perfume and a pair of silver hoop earrings. Hmmm.

"So what's new," she said casually, dragging a chair away from the table and sitting down as if they had all the time in the world to catch up. Charlie was busy putting the goodies in a plastic container, but she'd glanced at the clock twice since Lillian had arrived.

"Not much." Charlie aimed a careful smile at her and crouched down to pet Gloria, whose skinny dachshund tail wagged furiously. "How was business today?"

"Aside from caffeine addicts, not great," Lillian admitted. She traced a groove in the old tabletop with one fingernail. "No one's buying books in this economy, even before Christmas, so I left Jamie to close up." She looked up and caught Charlie's eye. "Now tell me, what's with the Shalimar?"

"The . . . ?" Charlie blinked in confusion, and when Lillian lifted an eyebrow and mimed spritzing herself with perfume, she gave a startled laugh. "Oh. The perfume. I . . . well, I just felt like . . . smelling pretty," she finished weakly. Then she frowned. "Is it too much? It's too much, isn't it?"

Lillian rolled her eyes. "Of course not. And the earrings are lovely, by the way. But what's the occasion? Come on, you need to give your friendly neighborhood crone some juicy gossip to cackle over."

Charlie glanced at the clock again and bit her bottom lip before schooling her expression into disapproval. "Gah. I hate that word and when did it crawl into the language?"

"It was a Wicca thing," Lillian said. "You know, books on that were hot sellers for a while. Now we can't give them away. Hoo hah. On to the next trend."

"Well, you're far from being a crone, so stop being silly. Anyway, it's nothing juicy. It's . . . well, it's sort of a long story, actually."

Lillian sat back easily, folding her arms over her chest. "I have all the time in the world."

Charlie groaned, but just then the doorbell

rang. Gloria raced toward the front of the house, barking happily. Charlie followed, Lillian close behind her, hushing the dog.

She grabbed Gloria up into her arms as Charlie opened the door, and when she saw who was on the other side, she was a little surprised her friend hadn't gone farther than perfume and silver hoops.

"Hi, Sam. Come on in," Charlie said, holding the door open for a tall sandy-haired man in faded jeans with the sexiest blue eyes Lillian had seen in a very long time. "This is my friend and neighbor Lillian Bing."

Sam looked surprised to find Charlie had company, which possibly explained the way he was trying to pretend the paper-bagged bottle of wine in his hand didn't exist. Lillian bit back a grin as he offered his hand.

"Nice to meet you," he said, and she was glad to find his grip firm and strong. None of that fake delicacy men tended to use when they shook a woman's hand. "Sam Landry."

"Likewise. I'm dazzled," Lillian said, and set the wriggling dog down to sniff at his ankles. "This is Gloria, by the way."

An eyebrow lifted in surprise. "Gloria?" he said as he bent down to offer the dog his hand.

"As in Steinem," she told him evenly, and waited. Men generally responded one of two ways on that—who's that? Or, you're kidding, right?

Instead, Sam smiled. There was indulgence in the curve of his mouth, but his approval was genuine, too. "Nice," he said, and scratched behind the dog's ears before straightening up. "I had a dog named Salinger once."

She nodded. It was a start, and a good one. Charlie deserved a guy with a head on his shoulders, and it didn't hurt that Sam's head was easy as hell on the eyes.

"What's this?" Charlie asked, craning her head to look at the skinny brown bag still behind Sam's back.

"White merlot?" Sam said dubiously, and held it out.

Charlie was blushing hard now, and Lillian watched as she jerked her head toward the kitchen, motioning for Sam to follow.

Oh, Charlie. She didn't know Lillian well enough to understand that a measly ten feet, not to mention no real sense of propriety, would never keep her from eavesdropping.

"I thought we agreed this wasn't a date," Charlie hissed, and Lillian shook her head.

"We agreed it was a stakeout," Sam said easily, and set the bottle down with a definitive clunk. "You have a corkscrew, I hope? And glasses? Although drinking out of the bottle is totally a stakeout thing to do."

"Since when do you drink on a stakeout?" Charlie said, and in between trying to decide what on earth the two of them could possibly be staking out, Lillian heard the note of helpless humor in Charlie's tone. Aha. She clearly liked this guy already.

With an unexpected stab of protectiveness, Lillian inched closer to the kitchen door. She hadn't known Charlie long, outside of the few times Charlie had visited the island with her parents or spent a weekend now and then with May, but Lillian was already fond of the adult she had become—her shy smile and her sneaky humor and, not for nothing, the way she had welcomed Lillian into her new home and her life without a second thought.

And Lillian had her own reasons for wanting Charlie to be a friend. Reasons that went back to the years before little Charlotte Jane Prescott had even been born.

"You know it's not really a stakeout, right?" Sam was saying, but his tone was gentle. "We can forget the wine, if you want. I just thought it might be a good way to pass the time."

"Tell you what. Let's mull it. A couple of cinnamon sticks, a little sugar—it'll really warm us up. Until the ghost shows up, the spare room is cold. And it'll make the whole house smell so Christmassy."

Lillian tried to put in her telepathic two cents. *Yes, but mulling wine burns off all the lovely Dionysian buzz. Drink it the way it is, you two.*

She hoped for Charlie's sake that she would make the most of this date. It wasn't just her own age range that had a shortage of single men. A stop into any of the local bars, not that Charlie seemed to drink, would show her that. Husbandly behinds, solid and square, were rooted to the stools, as the locals watched televised sports and muttered to each other. When it came right down to it, Lillian supposed there were a few bachelors among them, but they were still a sorry-looking lot, to a woman.

It wasn't often, if ever, on the Vineyard that a gorgeous guy showed up with a bottle of good wine, now was it? And why dirty up a pan, no matter how wonderful it made the house smell, when you could just drink together and be happy? Lillian bent over to scoop Gloria up when Charlie's cat Butch wandered down the stairs, tail waving in warning.

Lillian continued to scheme silently. They should pop the cork and pass the time talking, flirting, possibly kissing. Should she intervene? Hell no. She told herself not to be a busybody, even if young women these days were supposed to be so girls-gone-wild. Not bashful or hesitant like Charlie.

She flinched when she heard footsteps about to exit the kitchen, and backed into the front hall when Charlie appeared, fixing an innocent look on her face. "You know, I just remembered I have book group tonight at the store," she said easily. "I didn't read the book, of course, but at least I could be on time, right?"

Charlie frowned, blinking at her. "I thought you said . . ."

Lillian didn't have to answer, since Sam plunged in without waiting. "The store?"

"Pages, right in town," Lillian said. If the man

liked Salinger, he was clearly a reader. "My own small contribution to the world of independent bookstores."

"Excellent. I'm glad there are a few left on the planet." Sam's grin stretched from ear to ear. "I'll have to stop in while I'm here on the island."

"That you will," Lillian agreed and retrieved her coat and hat, snapping her fingers for Gloria. "Come around anytime. Ask Charlie, I'm almost always there."

Charlie was still frowning, obviously suspicious, but she walked with Lillian to the door. "I like him," Lillian said under her breath when they stepped onto the front porch. "Have a glass of wine, honey. Have two."

"Lillian."

"Just a friendly suggestion," she said airily, and let Gloria lead her down the walk. "You have fun now."

And don't think for a minute I'm not going to make you tell me all about it tomorrow, she said to herself, and grinned into the cold night air.

Charlie closed the door behind her and found Sam lounging against the staircase wall, arms folded over his chest, as easy and confident as if he owned the place. She took the opportunity to give him a good onceover, knowing that the light from the kitchen reflected in the lenses of her glasses. He wouldn't know. So . . . he'd changed his shirt and he'd showered before he came over—his hair was still slightly damp.

He liked to live dangerously, she supposed. He could count himself lucky that it hadn't frozen on his head.

Whatever. This still wasn't a date. Not even earrings and makeup on her and a bottle of wine from him—and was that aftershave he was wearing?—made it a date. Especially when he looked like the kind of guy who never bothered with a second one.

"So do you want to go upstairs?" she found herself saying, and winced in the silence that followed. That hadn't come out right at all. "I mean, it's after dark now and I'm sure you don't want to be here all night. Don't you have Christmas shopping or something—well, I guess it's early for that, huh?"

Bah humbug. What an idiotic thing to say. He was here, not at the mall. She had to stop talking right now.

Sam was just smiling, sly as a cat—a huge, very sexy cat—and she fought a flush of heat that was centered far lower than her cheeks.

"Why don't we open that wine?" he said finally, and took her hand to lead her into the kitchen. "And no, I'm not doing any Christmas shopping now or later that doesn't involve the *click-click-click* of a mouse. You haven't even told me about yourself, really, how you ended up here, what you do." He shrugged when she frowned, pausing over the kitchen junk drawer, and said, "Background information for the article. Not that I wouldn't like to know anyway."

"Well, I told you I inherited the house," she said, and snatched the corkscrew away before he could take it out of her hand. She twisted the sharp end into the wine carefully. "It's been in the family since Cyrus Prescott built it, and the family wants to keep it that way. My aunt was the last in her generation—my dad died about ten years ago, and so did their sister. She never married, so there was only me."

"Only you?" Sam lifted an eyebrow in disbelief. "Really?"

"I have cousins. Somewhere." She shrugged, and the gesture seemed oddly delicate given her thin shoulders. "Why? Do you come from a family of thirteen or something?"

He laughed, watching as she deftly unscrewed the cork and popped it out of the bottle smoothly. "No, it's just my brother and me. But I do have cousins, like you."

She poured the wine and passed him a glass before stopping to take an appreciative sniff of her own. "This smells wonderful. So, you know, grapey."

He chuckled the second she thought what a dumb thing that was to say.

"I believe it is made from grapes," he said seriously. "I read that somewhere."

Charlie gave him an embarrassed smile. He was confusing her. "Right. I was just saying."

His eyes softened with good-natured humor,

although his angular jaw and the sharp slash of his cheekbones remained impassive, set firm. But there was no mistaking the warmth in his eyes.

She nodded, and leaned back against the counter, settling her hips comfortably as she cradled the bowl of her glass in one hand. "Anyway, nothing much in the way of immediate family. No one around here."

"Got it." He stared into his glass for a minute, dark brows knit in thought. "Your dad died pretty young, huh?"

She nodded. Ten years later and she still missed him. "He was much too young and it was completely unexpected. I guess it always is, though."

"What about your mom?"

Charlie smiled and met Sam's eyes. "She got remarried two years ago, finally. She still misses my dad, but she likes being married, having a partner. And Joe is a good guy. They live in a tiny town in the Berkshires."

Sam nodded, but something in his face had changed. The tension was subtle, but it made her wonder what his parents were like.

"Lillian brought some goodies from the bookstore," she said to break the sudden silence. "I'm not sure gingerbread goes with white merlot, but we can give it a try." She got out a plate and opened the container where she'd stored the sweets, arranging them more carefully than necessary to give herself something to do instead of looking at Sam, who was much too easy to look at.

She put the shortbread Santa next to a gingerbread woman, then hastily moved him between two gender-neutral lemon bars, not wanting to seem as if she was making a pathetic hint or anything.

This is business, she reminded herself. For him anyway. And this year she had no time to waste on romance, especially not if it meant pining for a guy who didn't even live on the island.

And pining was what she would end up doing, she thought as she slid the plate toward Sam. She couldn't make a relationship work with a normal man who didn't completely intimidate her, much less a guy like Sam. Who had probably been fascinating girls since elementary school. She could see him now, all fourth-grade swagger, holding court on the playground.

"Does she bring dessert often?" Sam smiled around a mouthful of lemon square, and Charlie had to resist the urge to lean over and wipe a smudge of powdered sugar off his chin.

"They opened a coffee bar in the bookstore," she explained, carefully cutting a blondie in half. "Sometimes she brings the unsold stuff home when she closes up."

"But she was going back for her book group," Sam pointed out.

"I guess the members bring their own snacks," she said faintly, looking at the floor. There was no book group tonight. Lillian had lit up like a Christmas tree when Sam arrived, and Charlie knew what she'd been thinking. And knew, too, that she would be pumped for the details tomorrow, and part of her hated to disappoint her new friend. At sixty-eight, Lillian was far from a prim old woman, but she was also the most sensible, straightforward person Charlie had ever met.

She'd almost rather invent something juicy to share with Lillian instead of admitting that she thought the house was haunted and had actually agreed to be interviewed about it. The more she thought about it, the sillier it all seemed.

Not that she didn't believe there was a ghost in this house. She did. But it hadn't shown up out of nowhere. Yet no one in her family had ever mentioned even the possibility of a spirit wandering through this old place. Not to each other, as far as she knew, and certainly not in public. Suddenly, she could imagine several generations of Prescotts turning in their proper New England graves, mortified and ashamed of her.

Damn Franny, anyway, she thought with a quick stab of remorse. One panicked phone call to her friend on the mainland about things going bump in the night, and look where it had gotten her.

Of course, nothing might come of it, anyway. She took the last mouthwatering bite of blondie and glanced up at Sam, who was polishing off a second lemon square with enthusiasm. He certainly didn't believe her, anyway.

But maybe that wasn't why Franny had told him, she realized with such a start that she almost lost her balance. She was always telling Charlie to get out more, to have a little fun. Maybe Franny had been sending the fun right to her door.

"Nice to have a friendly neighbor," Sam remarked, brushing off his hands and sitting back with his wine. "You haven't been here long, have you?"

"Well, Lillian has lived next door her whole life," Charlie explained. "She's actually known me since I was a child, when we came to visit my father's sisters, Aunt Margaret and Aunt May. Are you keeping track of all this?"

"Oh yeah."

She shot him a dubious look. "But I think we might have become friends, anyway. Lillian's kind of fascinating."

"I bet she is." Sam grinned and swirled the last of the wine in his glass thoughtfully. "And tell her thanks for the sugar fix."

Charlie laughed, the wine and the treats combined making her warm, a little giddy. Which was probably a bad thing. She wasn't going to convince Sam there was something supernatural going on in this house if she was lightheaded with alcohol.

But she didn't care about that, really, she reminded herself. And Sam was the one who brought the wine in the first place.

Which still made this seem like a date, honestly. The trouble was that she wasn't sure she cared to protest about that anymore.

"You want to head upstairs?" Sam asked, and she blinked in surprise. Date or no date, she wasn't ready for—

"To do a little ghost-watching?" he prodded gently, watching her face, and she sighed in relief.

"Right. Sure." God, this was exactly why she never drank wine. Or anything else. Every brain cell in her head slumped over and went to sleep.

"You mentioned you were writing a book," Sam said as he climbed the stairs beside her, carrying the wine and his own glass. "You could tell me about that while we wait."

She glanced over her shoulder as she opened the door to the spare room. "I don't know . . ."

"Hey, keeping quiet didn't help before," Sam pointed out, edging carefully past her into the dark room. "Where's the light?"

"Oh." She stopped on the threshold, struck by the thick blackness in the room, not alleviated by the dim light at the other end of the upstairs hall. "There isn't even a lamp in here. But doesn't turning on the light seem sort of wrong to you anyway?"

He was closer than she'd realized, huge and solid, and she could feel the heat of him when he spoke, his voice low and a little rough. "You want to sit here in the dark?"

She swallowed, her tongue darting out to wet her lips before she could think better of it. It sounded incredibly tempting when he said it that way. "I was thinking maybe I could get a candle?"

"You could do that." He tucked the wine under his arm and took her glass. "I'll wait here."

She nodded, her mouth suddenly too dry and her heart banging clumsily in her chest. When she stepped back into the hall, she didn't know if the flush of heat on her cheeks was due to a preliminary emanation of the ghost—or simply to the sinful promise in Sam's voice.

What was more, as she hurried along the hall and back downstairs to the kitchen she found herself fervently hoping it was the latter.

Chapter Four

Charlie Prescott was too pretty for her own good, Sam thought as he groped his way into the spare room. Too pretty, too shy, much too inexperienced unless his instincts were way off, and thus not his type at all. Except for the pretty part, but that was usually a given. He could be shallow as the next guy, and he knew it.

What was worse was that Charlie clearly didn't know how pretty she was, or she would have realized the earrings and the perfume were completely unnecessary. And unless he was mistaken, she had no idea that he was far more interested in sitting up here in the dark with her, hopefully close enough to at least rub shoulders, than in waiting for an apparition he didn't believe in to show up.

All of which was dangerous, and bad, and just plain wrong. He was on an assignment here, not on a date, and the whole reason he was working for the ridiculous rag that was *Scoop* could be chalked up to wanting the wrong woman.

He groaned as he passed a hand over his eyes, then pinched the bridge of his nose firmly. He needed to concentrate. Focus. And what he should focus on was the fact that no matter how pretty and adorably shy Charlie was, she actually believed that the old house she'd inherited was haunted. By a ghost. Which didn't exist, and which every sane person over the age of ten knew as well as they knew the boy wizard who'd battled the forces of darkness through, what, ten books, wasn't real, either.

Didn't make him want to kiss her any less, though. She had the sweetest mouth, deep pink and soft and shaped like a bow, and when she licked the taste of the wine off her lips, the temptation to do it himself was so strong he could feel it like an urgent flash of heat.

Ignore it, he told himself, inching across the room and stubbing his toe once on something hard and solid. When he reached the bed, he slid to the floor and leaned against the side, setting the wine and the glasses beside him. Sitting on the bed was a much more attractive idea, so that was obviously out.

Ghosts, he told himself when he heard Charlie's footsteps in the hall. Think ghosts. Doing the graveyard boogie. With crazy women.

Except Charlie didn't look crazy when she stepped into the room, shielding the trembling flame of a fat white candle with one hand. The soft gold light threw her features into relief, outlined the gentle curve of her cheekbones and the gleam of her teeth as she bit into her bottom lip in concentration.

Ghosts, he told himself firmly, sliding over to make room for her. Which was crazy.

She set the candle down carefully and sat down, keeping a good foot between them. Wrapping her arms around her knees, she smiled shyly at him. "Is there any wine left?"

More wine was such a bad idea. It really was. He poured her a new glass and handed it over.

"So tell me about your book," he said, trying to look at anything but her, which was hard since the candlelight created more problems than it solved. Like making her look beautiful, almost from another time, like a woman from an old, old photograph. What were those called? Daguerreotypes. Yeah.

But the candle didn't do much for the room, which smelled musty from age and disuse, and the layer of dust on the floor was visible even in the candle's tentative glow. "What's it about?"

She colored again—he could see that much even in the dim light. "It's probably going to sound silly."

"Try me," he said easily, and leaned back, relaxing, his arms folded over his chest.

"It's a children's book." She risked a glance at him. "I've been working on it for a while, and it's called *Tales of the Darkbriar*. When I inherited this place, I inherited enough money, with what I have saved, to take a year off and try to finish it."

He couldn't help it—his eyebrows went up before he could stop them. "Aha. It wasn't your last red pencil breaking, you'd just had it."

She nodded, and her smile was proud. "I did. I figured it was now or never, you know?"

"That's ballsy," he said, and caught himself with a laugh. "Brave, I mean. Sorry."

She smiled indulgently. "It's okay. It was . . . ballsy," she said, testing the word out on her tongue. "I can go back, maybe not to the same school where I taught for years, but somewhere. I'm a good teacher. But I've always wanted to write this book, see if I can finish it, and even try to get it published. So . . . that's what I'm doing." She shrugged, her slender shoulders lifting the soft fabric of her sweater.

Charlie Prescott, taking her life by the horns. He had to admit he was impressed. If someone had asked him five minutes after meeting her, he would have said she was probably the type who still lived at home with her mother and had taken up knitting at the age of eighteen. Too scared to taste life, too timid to venture out into the world on her own.

Of all people, he should have known that the surface of any story was usually the least instructive.

He nudged her calf with the toe of his shoe. "You still haven't told me what the book is about. What exactly is the Darkbriar? A plant? A place?"

She swallowed a mouthful of wine and set her

glass down, suddenly sheepish. "You're going to think it's weird," she said softly, and smoothed a wrinkle in the leg of her jeans.

He quirked an eyebrow at her. "It's the epic love story of a talking dog and a lost penguin with a drinking problem."

She laughed. "No."

"The mostly true adventures of a transsexual sword swallower in 1950s Brazil."

This time, she nudged his thigh with her knee, still grinning. "Maybe next time."

"A vampire who's allergic to blood? A world made of shrimp? A cursed cubic zirconia that gives every girl who touches it a crush on David Hasselhoff?"

She was laughing helplessly now, and he found he liked the sound far too much. When she finally got it together, he sat back, pleased with himself. "Come on, spill."

"Okay, okay." She tucked a stray piece of hair behind her ear and tilted her head up at him. The candlelight glowed in her glasses, twin flames, and without thinking he reached out and took them off.

She opened her mouth in surprise, flinching. He studied her face without the wire frames, the long lashes sweeping her cheeks as she blinked at him, and laid a hand over hers gently. "I couldn't see your eyes," he said simply.

"Oh." Her voice was faint. "Okay."

"Tell me," he reminded her, and left his hand

where it was over hers, small but warm and sturdy beneath his palm.

She took a deep, shuddering breath, staring at their hands. "It's a children's book," she began finally. "About twins, a boy and a girl, who move to the country to live with a friend of their mother's after they're orphaned. She's a little distant, not very comfortable with them, and most of the time they're left on their own to explore this huge old house in the middle of nowhere . . ."

He was running his thumb over the back of her hand in a lazy circle when he realized she'd let the sentence trail off, her voice slipping into a whisper. And then he felt it.

She was staring at him, eyes wide and amazed, and he couldn't believe it, but he could feel it. Heat, a goddamn wall of heat pressing in against him that hadn't been there a moment ago. His lungs suddenly felt soupy, and his eyes burned with it, as if he'd opened the door to a blast furnace.

Charlie twisted her hand up to clutch his wrist, hanging on. He stared at her, sweating already, amazed that this was real, actually happening just the way she'd described it. That she had been through it before, all alone, and hadn't freaked out, hadn't run screaming from the house, hadn't simply passed out from the sheer intensity of the temperature shimmering the air around them. Even the candle blazed brighter, feeding on it.

The chill bleakness of December, a chill that had clung to this room, utterly vanished.

Her fingers tightened and he dropped his eyes to watch, feeling the sharp bite of her nails in his wrist, and then realized why she was doing it. There was more. More than just the heat. Under its surface, a ripple, a vibration, was something else.

And it was . . . need. A hi-we-just-met-but-I-think-I-love-you kind of need that made a man back a woman into a wall and kiss her until she was breathless, enjoy her mouth until it was swollen and red, lick into her to memorize the way she tasted, the way her tongue slid along his own.

Yeah. He gulped in a breath, lifting his gaze to Charlie's again, watching as she swallowed, the pulse in her throat beating so wildly he could see it even from here, even in the dull glow of the candlelight.

He could picture it all then, reaching for her, laying her back on the floor, stripping her sweater off and then her bra, filling his hands and his mouth with her skin, her breasts, swallowing her sighs and sobs as she trembled underneath him, sliding his fingers into her if she wanted that, claim her when she was ready . . . he was already edging closer, one hand cupping her cheek when he heard the growl.

It cut through the heat in a scary way, and the temperature dropped in its wake, a blast of pure ice. His breath hung in the air now, a thick, visible frost, and before he could even process what was happening, another strange growl ripped through the silence and the candle's flame wavered and flickered out.

"Sam," Charlie breathed, and then she was skidding sideways, out of reach, her wineglass hitting the floor as something solid slammed him into the bed. His shoulders hit with a dull thud, and it wasn't possible, couldn't be real, but the force of the blow was palpable, the heel of a hand connecting with his breastbone. He rocked back, gasping, as Charlie screamed, and just like that the cold melted away.

But he could still feel the icy outline of a handprint on his chest.

"Sam, are you okay?" Charlie was crawling toward him in the dark—the brittle chatter of breaking glass on the hard floor was followed by her hand on his thigh, small and shaking.

"I'm fine," he managed, and hated the way his voice shook, stripped down to nothing more than a husky whisper. He pulled her closer, hands on her shoulders, on her cheeks, grateful for the warm solidity of her. "What the eff just happened here?"

"I don't know." Her voice was trembling, and he tugged her up against him until her cheek rested on his shoulder. A fine shiver rippled through her as he stroked down her back. "That's . . . that's never happened before, I swear."

He swallowed, willing his heart to stop pounding. This was absurd. He was shaking like a little kid afraid of the monster under the bed, and he had never been that kid in the first place. Not to harp on it—he had to wonder why he'd needed to reassure himself as often as he had since arriving at Charlie's house—ghosts were bullshit, pure and simple, and he'd known that even when he was a child. Dead was dead, and ghosts were just projections of people's neurotic fears—or made up to frighten people, draw in tourists, add an air of mystery to an abandoned lighthouse or a run-down inn, give college kids a way to spook each other and snake a protective arm around a girl on a dark night.

But he'd felt that blast of air, the force of the hand pushing him backward—away from Charlie.

Right after the heat, as a matter of fact. He sat up straighter, arm still tight around Charlie's shoulders. Right after he'd reached for her, clutched in the tight fist of that heat, that need, that over-whelming drive to touch her, taste her, own her . . .

"Come on," he said gruffly, shaking her loose and getting to his feet. He took her hand and pulled her up against him, keeping her close. "Down-stairs. Now."

Well, she'd wanted to prove to Sam that there was a ghost in the house, Charlie thought as she sank into a chair at the kitchen table.

She just hadn't imagined the proof would be so unquestionable.

Sam was pale, pacing, and somehow furious.

He'd held onto her like she was about to break the whole way down the stairs, fingers digging into her upper arm until she'd squeaked a little in discomfort. And then he'd only loosened his grip instead of letting go.

Not that she could blame him, really. The first day she'd felt the ghost's presence in that room, she'd sat down hard on the floor, mouth gaping like a goldfish, blinking in some ridiculous combination of shock and fear and disbelief.

Which wasn't too far from what she was feeling now, actually. Her heartbeat had finally slowed down to a reasonable gallop, but she was as shaky and winded as if she'd run a mile on the empty winter beach. Her legs were rubbery, and she was still hot all over, shivering in the cool air despite her sweater.

Upstairs in that room, that had been more than just unexplained heat. More than the unexplained heat she'd felt before, at any rate. A lot more.

And it wasn't just the heat this time. It was something like a powerful inclination to do what came naturally. Starting with crawling into his lap and threading her fingers through his hair.

But it was more than that, a voice in the back of her head whispered. *And you know it.*

She had seen something that was almost like frames from a movie, disjointed, flickering in and out the way the candle did. Flashes of bodies half-wrapped in red velvet, naked skin gleaming, mouths open and wet against each other, hands clutching, stroking, tracing need into the gentle slope of a bare breast, the sense of love fully realized in a physical way.

She shivered, remembering it, and crossed her arms over her chest. That had definitely never happened before. She would have remembered that.

Sam's hand on her shoulder startled her out of her thoughts, and she couldn't help flinching at the sudden weight of it there. When she turned her face up to him, his eyes were dark, the pupils still blown, and his jaw was set hard.

"You said you'd never felt that cold before," he began, and pulled out the chair next to hers, finally sitting down. "Is that right?"

"Never," she said softly, and let him take her hand. He held it between both of his, clasping loosely now, as if the easy touch was enough to connect them.

Or maybe simply to reassure himself that she was all right, she realized. This was strangely comforting.

"You heard the . . . growl, right?"

She nodded, blinking up at him. It hadn't even sounded human.

"And you saw it . . . push me?" *Away from you* hung there unspoken, but she knew it as well as he did. She nodded again.

"And the . . . heat," he went on, carefully now, his gaze sliding over her face. "Was it like what you'd felt before?"

"Mostly," she said slowly. It was so hard to look

at him now, because she knew what was coming. He'd felt it, too. She swallowed hard, wondering how to explain it, or if even she had to.

"But there was more, wasn't there?" Sam said, and ducked his head lower to look her in the eye. "More than just the . . . the temperature?"

She nodded, trying to ignore the way her pulse raced. "It did seem stronger. Maybe it hit the eggnog again on the way up. The ghost or ghosts could be adding more whiskey or something. I'll have to check."

"Yeah. You do that," he whispered.

He was so close, so warm, and she could remember the way he'd touched her cheek, strong fingertips grazing the curve of it, learning its shape as he leaned in closer, as close as he was right now . . .

"Charlie."

She'd been staring at his mouth, she realized with a jolt, imagining it on hers, hot and demanding.

"You too?" His voice had dropped to a rough whisper. "Got that feeling, like you were watching—"

She made an inarticulate noise and held up her hand before he could say it, cheeks burning. "Yes. Like that."

"But that never happened before?"

She shook her head. God, it was so hard to look away from his eyes, the understanding there, as if he knew exactly what two bodies locked together so passionately felt like, as if he'd been about to pin her to the floor upstairs and show her . . .

"Charlie."

She'd watched his mouth move, watched her name form, and he was still talking, she realized.

"We should talk about this," he said, and his lips were so close to her cheek, she felt the words before she heard them.

She nodded again, felt him rest his forehead against hers lightly, barely brushing.

But when he caught her chin in his fingers a moment later and dragged her mouth up to his, that gentleness was gone.

And Charlie didn't mind at all.

Chapter Five

Charlie tasted like wine and sugar, and Sam licked into her mouth without hesitation. He was hot all over, his skin too tight, and he was hard already—no, still—and part of him knew it was just a side effect, whatever had happened upstairs lingering in this heat between them, but he didn't care.

Whatever was going on here was too astonishing to even consider. Charlie couldn't have set up a con on this scale, and there was no other explanation. Not one he was going to accept, anyway.

And he wanted Charlie. Had wanted her since sometime during her little rant about not being a spoiled heiress this afternoon, with her not-gem-encrusted shoe just short of stamping the floor in frustration.

His desire wasn't smart and it wasn't professional, but he didn't care about that either, not right now. She tasted good, felt good, and she was willing and hungry under his hands.

He pulled her roughly into his lap until she straddled his thighs, and then he ran his hands underneath the back of her sweater. She was so smooth, so soft, and he let his fingers trail over her back as he kissed her, tongue slowly exploring her mouth.

"We were . . . going to talk," she murmured against his lips as she threaded her fingers into his hair.

"Later," he said, licking along her jaw and taking the edge of her earlobe between his teeth.

"Later works," she breathed, and pressed harder against him. Her breasts were firm and sweet, and he could feel the rigid pressure of her nipples even through her sweater, his shirt.

He didn't do this. Well, he did this, sure, but he was usually a little more prepared for it. There was usually at least a couch, if not a bed, a good meal and some decent wine—okay, so he'd handled that part. But he'd never done the deed with only a few hours' acquaintance and some kind of freaky supernatural experience as a backdrop.

And yet here he was with Charlie on his lap, the unforgiving wood of a kitchen chair behind his back, and they were kissing like a couple of teenagers with the house to themselves for only a few minutes more.

They should stop, he thought, unhooking her bra and running his hands around the front of her to slide his hands under the cups, palm the warm, silky fullness of her breasts. They should stop now, before things went too far. Really. They barely knew each other, and he would bet folding money, a lot of it, that Charlie didn't do this kind of thing. Ever. Even after a lot more wine. He happened to glance at one of the Christmas cards, not liking to be watched by the big-eyed, green-capped elves on it. Okay, they were two-dimensional but he wasn't taking any chances, not after what had happened in the attic. Sam flipped the holiday card down on its face and returned his attention to her.

Then she made another inarticulate noise deep in her throat when his thumbs coasted over the firm tips of her nipples, and suddenly he forgot about stopping. He tightened his arms around her and pushed to his feet, laying her out on the wide, worn table. A piece of the day's newspaper slid away to one side; a straw basket holding a few ripe bananas skidded in the other direction with a muted whisper of wicker on wood.

He pushed her sweater up, exposing a wide swath of pale skin flushed hot with need, and she shivered. When she arched beneath his hands, she tipped her head back, and he found himself licking and biting at her throat, messy, open-mouthed kisses and sharp nips that made her tremble and hold onto him, her fingers digging into his shoulders.

God, he wanted her. Wanted all of her, right now, right here, naked and shaking and clinging to him. Wanted to watch her break open, swallow those soft, needful noises with his mouth, and stroke her back down until she was pliant and boneless in his arms.

The shrill ring of the phone cut through the silence, and Charlie stiffened beneath him. They both froze, panting, and Sam loosened the fingers he had tight against her hipbone, holding her in place. The moment was shattered, and for a second they simply stared at each other, trying to breathe.

"I should . . ." Charlie started, swallowing the rest of the sentence. Her eyes were huge, only a thin ring of brown visible around the blown pupils.

"Yeah," Sam said, straightening up, trying not to shudder. He was strung taut, aching and hard, and as Charlie pushed up to her elbows and wriggled off the table, he could suddenly see what the two of them must have looked like.

Scrubbing a hand over his face, he took a step back and helped her to her feet. She was shaky, all right, and her hair was wild around her shoulders, her recently replaced glasses sitting crooked on her nose. So sexy.

What the hell was he doing?

He waited while she stumbled across the kitchen to get the phone, dropping into the chair he had abandoned just minutes earlier. He barely registered her soft, breathless "Hello?" into the receiver.

This was crazy. Almost as crazy as a ghost, he told himself, and choked back a desperate laugh.

Charlie hung up the phone and turned around, smoothing her sweater into place and pressing her lips together. They were swollen, deep pink, evidence of his teeth and his mouth right there, and his dick twitched in recognition.

And interest. Yeah, definite interest.

"My friend Franny," Charlie said. She was blushing again, and more than anything he wanted to grab her up and kiss her, stroke her hair until she was soft and needy in his arms again. "I'm sorry about that, but she—"

"Hey." He closed the distance between them and pulled her against him. "No need to apologize. I should be the one doing that."

"Sam . . ."

He held firm, despite the breathy sound of her voice, muffled against his chest. "I'm going to go now," he said carefully, and put her away from him so he could look her in the eye. "But I'd like to come back tomorrow. So we can . . . talk. If that's all right."

She nodded, and he ducked down to kiss her, just once.

"You sure you're going to be okay here?" He jerked his head in the direction of the room upstairs. Christ, maybe he should take her with him.

But she was nodding, completely calm now. "I'll be fine," she said, and she sounded more certain of herself than she had all night. "Really."

He wavered for a moment, liking the feel of her hips under his hands, the smell of her, sweet and light and somehow spicy, but she set her jaw and finally wriggled out of his grasp.

"I'm a big girl," she said firmly, and he realized her blush had faded. "I'll be fine."

But as he kissed her good-bye, he wondered if she was talking about whatever had happened upstairs in that shrouded room—or what had almost happened right there on her kitchen table.

An hour later, dressed in a pair of loose flannel pajamas with a candy cane print, Charlie stood in front of the mirror over her dresser and touched her lips with one shaking finger. They were still flushed, slightly pouty, almost bruised. Her hair looked as if she hadn't combed it in a week, and her cheeks were still hot pink. Her throat, too. Or was that . . . ? She squinted, ran a careful fingertip over the faint purple mark where her neck met her shoulder. Hey, she actually had a hickey.

She'd never realized the evidence of kissing could be so, well, visible. Then again, she'd never kissed anyone quite the way she'd kissed Sam Landry.

Her knees wobbled a little just thinking about it. The two of them, clinging to each other, fused with fever-heat and need, on her kitchen table, for heaven's sake. If the phone hadn't rung when it did . . .

She took a step backward and sank into the overstuffed easy chair she'd brought from her old apartment in Providence. Butch yowled in protest, and she whirled around to catch him streaking across the room, all offended dignity and flickering striped tail. He sniffed and curled up in the bay window, studiously ignoring her.

"Sorry, buddy," she said faintly. She didn't sound quite like herself in the quiet room, but she didn't feel quite like herself, either, so that made a certain kind of twisted sense.

Charlotte Prescott didn't kiss strange men in her kitchen. Charlotte Prescott didn't kiss strange men anywhere. In fact, Charlotte Prescott had last kissed a man . . . She slouched into the chair as she thought back, surprised at how long it took her to figure it out. She hadn't kissed a man in almost two years. Her eyes widened as she realized how long it had been, and how little she had noticed.

Even so, she'd never done anything close to what she had done tonight with Sam. Nothing so frantic, so soon. She'd never even done anything like that in college, which was sort of the whole point of college, if you believed people like Franny, at least.

There had to be a reason for it. Outside of Sam being mouthwatering, of course. She'd met a few good-looking men in her life and she'd never jumped one of them that way.

Then again, she hadn't done the initial jumping, had she? She stood and crossed back to the mirror, removing her glasses to lean closer to the glass and study her reflection.

She wasn't anything much, really. At least she didn't think so. Plain light brown hair that hung straight down to her shoulders, myopic brown eyes, a mouth that had always seemed unremarkable aside from the fact that it was a pleasant enough shade of pink, and a straight, sort of boring nose.

Not bad, really. Just not . . . the type of woman who drove a man crazy. She certainly never had before, anyway. David would probably swear to that under oath, in fact.

She stuck her tongue out at herself, and leaned her elbows on the dresser's cluttered surface. The thing was, she wasn't the only thing that had happened to Sam tonight.

Slipping her glasses back on, she padded down the hall barefoot, biting her lip. No, something else had taken place here tonight, and it had been a hell of a lot more than she'd bargained for. Coming to a stop beside the closed door to the spare room, she touched the knob with careful fingers, swallowing hard, her heart beginning to speed up, and then frowned.

There was nothing to be afraid of. She'd been living here for almost two months, and the most she'd ever felt was that strange, sensual heat, after all.

Okay, that wasn't entirely true. Once, down in the kitchen, she'd heard whispers, faint and papery, like leaves scratching at the wind, so distant there was no way to make out actual words. Twice she'd smelled lilacs in the hall upstairs, just outside the spare room, and the aroma had been both so strong and so far away, she'd been rocked backwards, trying to figure out where it was coming from.

And once, just once, when she was still half

asleep and stumbling from the bathroom back to her bedroom, she had seen a gauzy flash of white just inside the spare bedroom, insubstantial, but somehow carrying the unmistakable curves and bell shape of a woman's dress.

She shuddered then, a faint thrill of unease, and let her fingers slide away from the doorknob. Whatever had happened before, she had never once experienced that blast of cold air, or heard that rough, furious growl before tonight.

And she still wasn't sure she believed what she knew she had seen—something incredibly strong shoving Sam backwards into the side of the bed, so forcefully his head had rocked on his neck for a moment as the breath whooshed out of his lungs.

Something had happened in that room, and for the first time she wondered if it was possibly something too strange. It was a ridiculous thing to consider now, she realized, backing away from the door. Cute little cartoon Casper was the only happy ghost she had ever heard of, and he wasn't a very good example of the spirit world, now was he?

She hurried back along the dim, chilly hall to her bedroom, doing her best not to slam the door behind her.

Butch lifted his head and regarded her with sleepy indifference when she crawled into bed, flicking his tail when the comforter shifted beneath him. "You didn't like it the one time you felt the ghost," she told him with a frown, and rolled her eyes when he sniffed and leapt off the bed.

She snuggled down and reached for the book she'd left on the night table, but she couldn't concentrate. When she wasn't feeling that bitter, icy rush of air against her skin, she was back in the kitchen with Sam, the table biting into her spine and his mouth hot and demanding against hers, the muscles in his back rippling like water as he moved, his hair sliding thick and silky under her hands, and then she was flushed all over again and so restless she had to start the page of her book all over again.

She gave up when she'd read the same paragraph three times without registering a word of it, and turned off the light. There in the dark, there was nothing but the fitful wind outside and the house settling around her, faint creaks and groans as the old structure eased farther into its foundation.

She couldn't think about the spare room, not without the urge to pull the covers over her head like a frightened little girl. It wasn't any safer to think about Sam as she lay there in the dark, but it was certainly much more enjoyable.

Chapter Six

"You can't bring that in here," a woman with shockingly blond hair and a Reading is Fun button pinned to her blouse told Sam the next morning. He was only two feet inside the Edgartown Public Library, a tall takeout coffee in hand and his laptop bag over his shoulder, and it took a moment to realize she was talking to him.

And what she was talking about. His fingers tightened around the cup when she pursed her lips and lifted her eyebrows in disapproval.

"Right," he said, backing out and trying not to scowl.

"Shush," she answered reflexively, then turned to whatever it was she had been looking at on her computer monitor.

She looked as if she'd been ready to confiscate the cup, and if anyone tried to get between him and his caffeine this morning, they were going to get an earful.

He was almost certain there wasn't enough

coffee in the world this morning anyway. On his back in the too small, sickeningly antiqued room he'd booked at the Edgartown Inn, just two blocks away, he'd stared at the ceiling for hours last night.

Remembering the gut punch of that icy air, and the threatening growl rumbling through the room right behind it. The slow pressure of that sexual heat under his skin. The way Charlie had tasted when he kissed her, the soft give of her skin under his palms, the breathless way her mouth had opened when he'd nipped at her collarbone and soothed the sting of the bite with his tongue . . .

Yeah, if he kept thinking about it now, he'd be up forever. In more ways than one, he thought with a silent groan. He hitched his bag up over his shoulder and set out down the street, the cup's warmth comforting in his hand. He just needed . . . more coffee. And research. Research would ground him, anchor him in the real world, not whatever freaky dimension he had wound up in last night in Charlie's house.

That hadn't been Frosty the Snowman who'd tried to knock him on his ass when he'd gotten too close to Charlie. But who—or what—had it been?

Her house was right around the corner he realized with a grunt of frustration. Not that he had meant to head in that direction. Not at all.

Of course, his feet weren't exactly turning around. What the hell?

A retiree with a golden retriever so white around

the muzzle it looked to be roughly as old as his owner walked by, smiling up at Sam from beneath the brim of a Red Sox cap. "Morning," he called cheerfully, the day's newspaper folded beneath one arm.

Sam grunted and kept walking. Everything about Edgartown was straight out of a postcard, glossy and neat. Even the bleak winter weather didn't take away from the neat Victorians lined up like dollhouses, sporting tidy Christmas wreaths and tasteful garlands. This wasn't the kind of town that went for big inflatable displays or tons of outdoor lights and nodding white-wire reindeer. Of course, one gust of the wind off the Atlantic would probably blow an inflatable Santa all the way up to the North Pole.

Even the locals were straight out of central casting, from the strict, shush-a-matic librarian to the old-timer walking his dog, for God's sake.

And that was before you got to the cliché of the haunted sea captain's house.

He turned up Morse Street before he reached Cottage, determined to finish his coffee even though it was freezing out and get his head on straight before he headed over to Charlie's. Calling her first would be safer anyway. If he knocked, he knew what would happen. She would answer, glasses sliding down her nose and her hair tucked behind her ears, blushing and shy, and he would . . . well, he would tackle her right there in the front hall and kiss her breathless, and that was probably still a bad idea.

Every part of his body aside from his brain disagreed about it being a bad idea—in fact, a couple of parts seemed to consider getting his mouth on Charlie's was a damn good plan—but he was determined to ignore their protests for now.

It was only ten o'clock in the morning. He had some self-control. Not much, but some.

He was downing the last of his coffee when he heard, "Well, if it isn't Sam Landry. Good morning to you."

When he looked up, Lillian Bing was leaning in the doorway of a shop just a dozen feet away, arms crossed over her chest and Gloria the dachshund was circling her feet, tail wagging frantically. Above the woman's clipped silver hair, a hanging shingle swung in the wind off the water. The word Pages was painted there across a simple graphic of an open book.

"Lillian. Morning."

"You don't sound completely caffeinated yet," she said with a knowing smile. She was squinting in the weak sunshine, one hand up now to shield her dark gray eyes. "Come on in and I'll fix you up."

He followed her into the store, nose twitching at the combination of new books, vintage volumes, coffee, leather, and what he was pretty sure was patchouli. He could picture Lillian as a hippie, he realized, imagining her hair before it had turned pewter, maybe long and braided down her back. She was about the right age, and she had the turquoise and silver jewelry to lend at least a little credence to the theory. And she'd named her dog after Gloria Steinem, who wasn't a hippie but from back in the day, for sure.

"So, a bookstore," he said, wandering through the stacks up front, making sure his voice carried to Lillian, who'd disappeared behind a counter at the far wall, but not before catching her tunic top on a bristly garland of spiky red and green. There were Christmas-themed doodads all over the place, including a retro Rudolf with a blinking bulb for a nose.

The place wasn't big enough so that being heard was a problem, although every inch was packed with shelves, each of them crammed with books. Every few feet, the ones that didn't fit were piled on the floor.

"You noticed," Lillian said amiably. "How do you like your coffee? And do you want French roast, Blue Mountain, or house blend?"

"Blue Mountain," Sam said approvingly, and ran his fingers over a fresh stack of the new Chuck Palahniuk novel. "And I'll fix it if you don't mind."

"Did you eat breakfast? I have scones and pumpkin muffins. Mind if I mom you?"

"Not really. Thanks. I'll take a muffin," Sam said, and found his way back to the counter, stepping over Gloria twice and setting his laptop bag down in an ancient leather easy chair the color of faded tobacco. "This is a great place."

"It works for me," Lillian said easily, sliding a large paper cup across the counter at him and taking his empty, tossing it neatly at the trash can. She took a muffin from the pastry case with a pair of tongs and set it on a plate. "I've had it since . . . wow, let me think, 1979."

"Had it?" Sam asked, spooning sugar into his coffee and adding a healthy splash of cream. "Did you buy it?"

"I did." Lillian came around the counter with her own cup and dropped into the chair beside Sam's. The store was empty except for the two of them and Gloria, worrying a stray napkin across the floor with her nose. "I'd been working at the private school over in Falmouth, in the library, and when I heard the bookstore was for sale, I jumped."

"That's a big jump," Sam said, settling back in the chair. He took a deep, appreciative sniff of his coffee and smiled. "Librarian to small business owner."

"Well, I wasn't married, and I was tired of snotty kids who didn't know the difference between Jane Eyre and Dick and Jane, not that anyone's learned to read from those two little robots for a thousand years. Anyway, I've always liked books better than people." She sipped her coffee and looked up when the bell over the door jingled. "Morning, Tony."

A tall guy with a shaved head and three safety pins in each ear ambled up to the counter, black leather jacket crackling comfortably as he went. "Morning." He stopped and looked at Sam dubiously, mouth twisting into a frown. "Coffee?"

"Help yourself," Lillian said with a fond smile. "I'm too comfortable to get up."

Tony shrugged and walked behind the counter, as if self-service wasn't a surprise.

"A regular?" Sam said quietly, turning to Lillian.

She nodded. "One of a few. It's a little rough in the off season, but they help." She put her cup down on the table between their chairs, and propped her chin in one hand. "So what brings you to the Vineyard, Sam Landry?"

He heard the unspoken question: *What are you doing with Charlie Prescott?*

Lillian didn't strike him as the maternal type necessarily, but he didn't blame her. He wasn't from the island, he'd shown up at Charlie's with a bottle of wine, if not flowers, and if Lillian had happened to be watching out her window last night, she'd seen him practically staggering out of Charlie's place.

"I'm with . . ." He trailed off, hating to say the name of the magazine and stared at a point across the room instead of looking at Lillian. "*Scoop.* I'm writing a piece on haunted houses of the New England coast."

Lillian barely swallowed a snort of laughter, but he gave her credit for not laughing out loud. "That's . . . interesting," she said carefully, and picked up her cup to hide her smile behind its lip. "But what do haunted houses have to do with Charlie?"

He had opened his mouth to make a smart

remark to reply to her that's . . . interesting, and closed it just as quickly. "Uh, what?"

She blinked at him, and he felt a little bit like a slow five-year-old facing a mean teacher. "What do haunted houses have to do with Charlie?" she repeated, carefully enunciating, and he scowled at her.

"You don't know?"

"Know what?" she said with a huff of exasperation, setting her cup down again. Understanding dawned in those sharp gray eyes all at once. "Are you telling me Charlie thinks that house is haunted?"

He shifted uncomfortably in his chair, tightening his fingers around his cup. Charlie had seemed so adamant—as she apparently had every right to—and he had never imagined she wouldn't have mentioned her suspicions to anyone. Especially not Lillian, who seemed to be Charlie's closest new friend here on the island.

"Sam." Lillian's tone wasn't the kind anyone could ignore, and he swallowed back a protest.

"I don't know what I'm supposed to tell you," he said finally, and turned to her. Her eyebrows were lifted in disbelief—or was that anticipation?

Lillian dismissed him with a wave of her hand, ignoring Tony as he swore behind the counter when something crashed to the floor. "Don't be an idiot. If you're interviewing her about this, and you include her story in your article, the whole world's going to read about it when it's in print. Spill the beans, buddy."

"Hey, I'm not actually five, you know," Sam said irritably. He shook his head when Lillian made a face, and leaned forward, elbows on his knees. "She thinks the house is haunted, yes. And that the ghost or whatever it is has been glugging up her eggnog and whiskey. And apparently its presence is playing hell with the thermostat." He hadn't planned the next words out of his mouth, but once they hung there in the air between them, there was no taking them back. "And I think I believe her."

At eleven o'clock that morning Charlie groaned and pushed away from her desk, the chair's wheels squealing against the bare wood. She'd been up and at her desk since eight-thirty, despite only three hours and twenty-seven minutes of sleep, and in two-and-a-half hours she'd written only—she looked back at the computer screen—fourteen words.

Fourteen. Fourteen nonsensical, poorly strung together words that didn't even amount to a decent paragraph. In fact—she squinted at the screen again—one of the sentences was just a fragment.

It didn't make any sense. She'd been writing this book off and on, sometimes only in her head, for seven years. She knew the twins so well by now they might have been her own siblings. For years she'd been plotting the story and imagining settings, descriptions, the dangers the young hero and heroine would face when they explored the magical world she'd built for them. She knew this book inside and out, from the very beginning through every adventure to the end. Years of writing bits and pieces of it at the end of the day and on weekends and vacations had only gotten her so far, and she had been dreaming for a chance to sit down and finish the thing in one go.

But now she was stuck. And it was because all morning a whole new story had been crowding its way into her head, insinuating itself over every plot point and twist of the Darkbriar book.

She got up, twisting her hair into a loose knot on the back of her head and shoving a pencil through it to anchor it in place. Sometimes she could think more clearly when the loose length of it was up off her neck, but it didn't seem to be working this morning. She'd already twisted it up and taken it down a dozen times as she paced the length of the small room, running her fingers over her bookcases, stopping to change the angle of the framed photos on her desk, plumping the pillows in the easy chair in the corner.

It was procrastination, pure and simple, but she couldn't help it. Not today, anyway. Usually the simple action of moving around, getting the blood flowing, helped her figure out a problematic scene or the best way to describe a setting, but this morning she couldn't even concentrate on her characters.

Because two completely new ones were shouting at her, waving frantically like shipwreck survivors, demanding that she write about them instead. They were adults, for one thing, nothing like her adorably gawky protagonists, and what was more, they were adults who had no interest in magic or the enchanted countryside or anything aside from each other.

In fact, they never got out of their fictional bedroom. The scene between them echoed in her head, as if it was being written word by word in her imagination then and there.

"You are shamefully bold." With his back pressed against the wall, Daniel growled rough in his throat when Temperance slid her pale hands over his hips and pressed a kiss to his collarbone. Even through the worn white muslin of his shirt, her lips were warm, firm, a sinful promise.

"I believe you approve," she murmured. Her skirt whispered against the floor as she moved, pressing the slender length of her body against him, stretching up on her toes to wind her arms around his neck. *"You're a shy one, Daniel. If I don't ask for what I want, I'm not at all certain to receive it."*

"No question of that anymore, love." He slid a hand into her hair, knocking the pins loose, shaking the dark, silky length of it out over her shoulders. She smiled at him, satisfied as a cat, and turned her face up to him for a true kiss.

The first was always the sweetest, he thought

as he licked into her mouth. It wasn't the way she tasted, though he loved that, oh he did, yes indeed. It was her eagerness, the way she opened to him so easily, going boneless against him, letting him take what he wanted. She always tasted faintly of tea, but of need, too. He'd come to believe the bittersweet flavor there on her tongue was the soul of urgency.

It always surprised him when she remembered herself, pressing harder against him, and began to make her own demands. Temperance had been sadly named, he would swear that on the Bible itself, even if his mother would have boxed his ears for the blasphemy. His Tempe knew nothing of moderation, not when they were alone together this way, nothing but hands and mouths and the hot pulse of desire thrumming in their blood.

"We have all afternoon," Temperance whispered now, her breath hot against his throat and her fingers tight on his hips, ten distinct points of pressure. "I sent Agnes into town on a dozen fool's errands, and my father will be tied up for hours with his solicitor. The house is ours."

He pulled her closer, tighter, pressing the hard length of his erection into her belly. She sighed in response, as if nothing mattered but the two of them here like this, aching for each other until there was nothing for it but to be naked and slick in the tangled sheets of her bed.

She sighed when he turned her around and fumbled with the buttons marching up the back of her bodice in neat order. His hands trembled, always did—this moment, right here, when she was pliant, offering herself to him, always undid him. That she trusted him with her body, that she wanted him, his hands on her, his tongue, his mouth, him, was always a revelation in this moment, when he was stripping away her dress. She never hesitated, never played coy, not even the first time, when he had braced for a slap after every rough, demanding kiss he'd stolen in the shed down behind the house.

When the dress slid away from her shoulders, she stepped out of the puddle of sheer white lawn and let him untie her lacy corset cover and drawers. They fluttered to the carpet, white on blue, and she curled her hands around the bed's foot rail, bending forward. Her bare bottom was creamy, smooth, and he let himself brush against it as he reached for her corset. It took careful fingers to unfasten the row of tiny hooks, and to stop himself from kissing every inch of skin he exposed. When he had tossed the corset into a chair and she was naked, she turned back to him, pale and soft everywhere, except for her hair, tumbling in a dark, glossy spill over her shoulders and brushing the white curves of her breasts.

"Danny," she whispered, as if it were the only word she knew, and opened her arms to him, bare and perfect against the busy background of the room's wallpaper, the grand canopy that arched over her bed like a crown. He let her undress him, until he was as naked as she was, achingly hard, his erection proud and flushed

*as it strained toward her, and then there was
nothing but the heat, flickering higher with each
touch, each kiss, until it blazed bright enough to
consume them.*

Hoo hah. Maybe she should just turn the thermostat back up to 72 and stop trying to be green.
Her body and her ecological conscience were
clearly at war.

She blushed just thinking about those lovers,
who'd pushed their way into her imagination
sometime last night. The things she'd imagined
them doing were, to put it mildly, definitely not
rated for general audiences.

Grabbing up her coffee mug, she headed downstairs, scowling. It was Sam's fault, obviously. The
man had scrambled her brain so thoroughly he'd
flipped some internal switch in her imagination
from "children's book" to "hot romance."

She walked into the kitchen and opened a can-
ister on the counter to spoon up fresh coffee for a
new pot. Between the lack of sleep and the love
scenes playing in her head all morning, she was
starting to feel a little strung out. She either needed much more caffeine or about two days' worth
of sleep.

*Or to finish what you started with Sam last night,
right there on the kitchen table,* a voice in her head
whispered, low and seductive. She was so startled
at the clarity of the image she dropped the used

filter on the floor, the sodden grounds landing with a disgusting wet plop on the polished wood.

She closed her eyes in frustration for a moment, and realized she could practically feel his big, strong hands on her, right here, right now. The slow, sensuous sweep of his tongue in her mouth, the hungry groan he breathed into her ear when he pulled her onto his lap.

Opening her eyes, she backed into the counter, flushed and breathing heavily. This was crazy. Okay, she thought he was gorgeous, she'd thought that the moment he walked through her door the first time yesterday morning, but she'd been attracted to men before, plenty of times. She'd never felt this, though. This urgent, inescapable desire to kiss him, touch him, taste him, everywhere.

Something had happened last night, something much more complicated than a couple glasses of wine and two people who didn't want to admit they were lonely, not in so many words. Maybe they had taken that what-say-we-chase-away-the-holiday-blues thing a little too far.

And it had started in that upstairs room, she thought, glancing at the ceiling as she knelt down to attack the mess on the floor with a paper towel. The soggy filter ripped, spilling more of the damp grounds across the wood when she tried to pick it up, and she groaned again.

The weird thing wasn't that she had heard the noises and felt the heat before without anything so intense happening. Charlie got up and went to the pantry for the whisk broom and the dust pan.

The weird thing was that she had never experienced anything like it in all the years she had come here before moving in.

Her father had grown up here, after all, and they'd come every summer when she was a kid. She'd loved packing her suitcase at home in Boston, carefully choosing which shorts and bathing suits to bring, laying out her sandals and flip-flops, whatever books she'd taken out of the library and either Emily, her well-loved, sadly shabby doll and the wardrobe her mother added to every Christmas, or her best colored pencils and a new drawing pad, depending on her age.

Most of her time had been spent on the beach, of course, running up and down the hot sand in her bare feet, splashing in the waves that lapped at the shore, digging for hermit crabs and building elaborate tunneled holes for the water to fill, since she'd never been any good at sandcastles. They always spent a week at the house, and sometimes she and her mother had stayed longer while her father went back to Boston, leaving them to putter around with Aunt May, making iced tea on lazy afternoons, watching the old TV in the living room in the evenings with bowls of popcorn or popsicles, depending on the heat.

They'd come to the house for Thanksgiving some years, too, and once for Christmas, when Aunt May wasn't up to traveling. And in all those years, Charlie had never once heard a ghostly whisper or felt anything other than the humid, salty heat of a summer afternoon on the island, or the drafty chill of a winter morning in a rambling old house with ancient windows.

She brushed the grounds and the torn filter into the dust pan and stood up to carry the whole mess to the garbage can, thinking back. She'd slept in the room that was now her office, but her parents had slept in the spare room. Of course, they never would have mentioned something as disturbing as feeling the presence of a ghost to a child, but once she was older?

Well, she knew what she would have said if she'd never seen or heard anything herself. She would have raised her eyebrows and wondered if they were getting prematurely senile.

Which wasn't fair at all, but at least it was honest. She had an active imagination—always had, according to both her mother and the yellowed notebooks packed away that contained pages of her first attempts at stories, more like extended daydreams—but it had taken feeling the ghost, hearing that papery whisper, to believe that such a thing as a spirit could actually exist.

It made her wonder about Aunt May, Aunt Margaret, the generations who had lived in this house before them. What had happened here, and to whom? Cyrus Prescott had built this crazy old place back in the last century, with its Victorian excess and gingerbread moldings and endless nooks and crannies, and it had been in the family ever since. Whatever had occurred here that might have caused a ghost to stick around, it had happened to someone in the Prescott family, or at least someone closely associated with them, which was a little disturbing, to say the least.

She filled a new filter with coffee, and set up the machine to brew, pondering everything she knew about the Prescotts, which suddenly seemed like not very much at all. She was so deep in thought as she put her few clean breakfast dishes away and waited for the fresh pot of coffee that the noise she heard a moment later caught her off guard.

It was just the wind, she thought, glancing over her shoulder at the empty room. Buttery sunshine slanted across the floor and the back window was a grid of bright squares, the morning sky captured in the glass. There was nothing off here, nothing scary or weird or unnatural at all.

And then there was. She froze, clutching a clean mug, as a sound rippled through the room, a crackling like crumpled paper, brittle with age. And just below it, the single, echoing word, barely audible: *Mine.*

Chapter Seven

Sam was just about to knock on Charlie's front door when it was flung open. Charlie stared at him, gasped in surprise, pale as a sheet, and took a step backwards.

She was shaking, Sam thought absently, and was inside with his hands tight around her upper arms before he even knew he was about to move.

"What's wrong? What happened?"

She shook her head and wriggled out of his grasp, pushing past him to get outside, without a jacket or anything. At least she was wearing those slipper-sock things. He followed, ignoring the open door but setting down his leather laptop bag on the clean gray-painted floorboards of the front porch.

"Charlie, talk to me." He took her arm and steered her into one of the Adirondack chairs by the railing, going down on one knee to look up at her. It was chilly out despite the bright sky and the sunshine—the wind off the water carried winter's chill. "What happened?"

She was still shaking a little bit, although he decided at this point that it was due more to the temperature than whatever had spooked her. He ran his hands down her arms as she got calmer, taking a while to raise her gaze to his. She was sheepish, a little scared, confused, and he wanted to make all of it go away. "What happened?" he asked again, more softly this time.

"I was in the kitchen, making a fresh pot of coffee, and I heard something," she said. Her voice was surprisingly steady despite the fine trembling that wouldn't quite stop, and the awful paleness of her cheeks.

"Heard what?" His knee was protesting the unforgiving surface of the floor, but he wasn't going to move until he knew what had happened.

"I thought it was the wind at first," she explained, and took a deep breath to steady herself. "I've heard things before, just once or twice, but it was always very vague, something I could almost pass off as the house settling or leaves rustling. But today . . ." She pressed her lips together, frowning hard, trying to decide how to explain. "In the past, I could tell there was a voice there, but it was too far away to really hear. Today I heard it, and it was just one word inside this strange . . . sort of crackling noise."

His pulse had kicked up, he realized, and he was gripping her arms so tightly he was going to leave bruises if he didn't relax. "What was the word?"

"Mine," she said simply. Behind her glasses, her eyes were huge, the soft, dark brown of them gleaming with amazement and the last faint tinge of fear. "That was it, just 'mine.' But the voice . . . it was so hard. I couldn't tell if it was male or female, because it was still so distant. But whoever it was, it didn't sound happy. Not pleased and proud, if you know what I mean. It was possessive. Determined."

She shuddered suddenly, and he let go of her arms to rise up and gather her against him. After one surprised, frozen moment, she slid her arms around his back and laid her head on his shoulder with a little sigh.

"It's silly," she said, the words muffled by his shoulder. He could feel the warmth of her breath through his parka. "I mean, I've heard and seen things, and last night I wasn't even this scared, really. I think it was just because I was alone, and it was so quiet in the house." She moved, trying to disentangle herself, but he held her tight.

"It's not silly," he said gruffly. "It's weird and, yeah, a little scary. Ghosts aren't supposed to be real, no matter how many believe in them. But I think the talking ones are more rare. After last night . . ."

She stiffened a little then, and he ran a hand down her back, soothing and steady. "Last night was an eye-opener. I'll admit it. That . . . growl was real enough, I can tell you that. And getting pushed around by something I can't see is not my idea of a good time. I don't blame you, babe. Not one bit."

He could feel her smile against his shoulder.

Of course, he could also feel her breasts through the simple white button-down she was wearing over her jeans, and smell the good, clean, girl-scent of her shampoo in her hair. The back of her bra was a gentle ridge beneath his hand, and he itched to unhook it, unbutton her shirt, twist her around so he could get his mouth on her, taste that sweet darkness on her tongue.

No.

They were on her front porch in broad daylight, on a frigid December morning, and he was ready to strip her down and take her right here. She didn't even seem to notice that she didn't have a jacket on, but if she caught pneumonia, it would be all his fault and—What the hell was this? He liked her, yeah, and he wanted to get to know her better in more ways than one, but this? This was crazy. This wasn't him. Not entirely, anyway. But he had to get her inside.

And control himself until she'd calmed down. He was pretty sure it wasn't her, either. Granted, he only knew enough about Charlie to fit on the head of the proverbial pin, but he was willing to bet money that she wasn't the type who would usually turn her head to find a man's mouth, hungry and hot, as if she'd read his mind.

As if she needed this just as badly as he did, right here and right now.

He couldn't argue the point, not right away. Not

with her tongue slipping in against his, wet and sweet, and her fingers twisting in the fabric of his shirt, holding on as he angled them closer. His knee was screaming, and his hips were aching from the uncomfortable position he was in, but right now it didn't matter. He kissed her harder, until it was all teeth and lips and tongue, messy and fast.

She broke away so suddenly, his head followed, his mouth eager to claim hers again, but instead of breaking away completely she was standing up. And dragging him with her, it turned out, her fingers hooked into his belt loops.

"Inside," she said. And they were. Just like that.

"Charlie," he breathed, and she just nodded up at him, cheeks hot with color, her mouth bruised dark pink from his kisses.

"Sam," she said, voice full of wonder and need and heat, and then they were kissing again, her arms around his neck. She was up on her toes to reach him better, and he was cupping her ass, bringing her closer.

God, he wanted her. Wanted all of her, naked and sweat-slick and needy beneath him, and he slid his hands up under her shirt, dragging his palms slowly over all that smooth, soft skin.

She wriggled closer, licking into his mouth with her hands on his face, holding him there, and he groaned out loud, sinking his fingers into the rounded curves of her ass, not even noticing they were in front of a window.

Just as someone called up from the sidewalk. "Hi, Charlie! Oh! Uh . . ."

They disentangled so quickly, Charlie stumbled, banging her knee on the wide wooden windowsill, and Sam swayed for a minute, trying to regain his balance without the warm anchor of her body against his.

"Hi, Isabel," Charlie called through the window, her hand at half mast in greeting. The woman who had spoken was about Charlie's age and pushing a sleek navy blue stroller, but instead of stopping she just smiled and hurried on as she called over her shoulder, "I'll, um, talk to you later!"

"Oh brother," Charlie groaned, sinking into an armchair and shivering all of a sudden. "We barely know each other, and now she probably thinks . . . I don't even know what she'll think now."

"Who cares," Sam said firmly. He took her hand and pulled her to her feet. She let him steer her away from the window. He dashed outside again and collected his laptop before it froze and the screen shattered, then shut the front door firmly behind them.

For a moment, they simply stared at each other, and Sam could feel the magnetic pull between them that made going right back to what they'd been doing the best and most sensible idea in the world. The temptation was clear on Charlie's face, too—she was breathing hard, her cheeks still hot with color, and her lips were still parted, still slick with their kisses.

One step, he thought. If he took one step toward her, she'd be in his arms, and then they'd be . . . well, not upstairs in her bed, that much was pretty clear. She'd be lucky if they made it to the couch instead of right here on the floor of the entry hall.

Which was wrong. Wrong. Hot, yeah, definitely, but it couldn't happen right now, not like this, not when he didn't know what the hell was going on and why the two of them were like a couple of animals in heat around each other.

It had to be the house. Or whatever was in the house. Whatever strange entity had taken up residence here. Had to be.

He tightened his fingers around the strap of his bag and set his jaw. Charlie was waiting, eyes troubled behind her glasses, her chest still faintly heaving. "Get your coat," he ground out with effort. "We have some research to do."

"This is a lot less fun than researching faery rings and the English moors," Charlie said two hours later at a table in the back of the library, idly flipping the pages of a book on the whaling history of Martha's Vineyard.

She glanced up, looking around. Whales were popular in these parts, maybe a little too popular. There were Christmas cutouts taped to the ends of the tall shelves, and one of them was a whale in a Santa hat, pulling a sea-sleigh piled high with gifts for the good little boys and girls of Edgartown. Awww.

Sam shot her an annoyed look. "Do you want to figure out what's going on in that house or not?" He was sprawled in a curving, solid oak chair on the other side of the table, catty-corner from her—as far away as he could get and still be at the same table, she thought, and sighed.

Which was for the best, obviously. Especially here. She was fairly certain that the staff of the Edgartown Public Library would not approve of public displays of affection in the reference section, or anywhere else.

And keeping her hands off Sam was proving more and more difficult to do, no matter where they were, it seemed.

Shoulders bumping as they'd set out from her house to the library, she'd taken Sam's hand without thinking twice. In the just-above-freezing morning air his hand had been so warm, so strong, and when he had let his thumb trace lazy circles on the back of her hand, the rush of heat in her belly was a shock. They were holding hands, for heaven's sake, not kissing, not . . . well, practically climbing all over each other the way they had been on her porch, in front of her entire neighborhood.

She blushed again just thinking about it, and Sam scowled. "Keep reading," he muttered and, judging by the way he slid further down in his chair, adjusting his position, she knew he was still feeling it, too. Arousal. Need.

She turned back to the book lying open on the table in front of her. It dated back at least a century and a half, and it was yellow with age and stiff with disuse. Which had as much to do with the author's dry-as-dust style as the topic of whaling which had bored her to tears the minute she'd gotten three chapters into Moby Dick back in college, come to think of it. If she read one more laundry list of a ship captain's household inventory from 1856, she was going to scream. Or possibly fall asleep right here in the library.

"Look, the idea is to find out anything we can about the Prescotts," Sam said without preamble. He'd explained the point of this unexpected research trip four times already, and she was beginning to believe he was talking just to keep himself from leaping across the table and kissing her, judging by the look on his face.

Which was hot and bothered in the extreme, she thought, answering heat flooding up from her chest and into her cheeks. He'd pushed his hands into his hair so many times, it was spiked up every which way, and those blue eyes were still dark, a thin ring of warm blue ocean around the black of his pupils.

She turned back to the book in determination, flipping to the next page. The point of this excursion was to find out whatever they could about her family's history, about the house itself, if and when anything strange had happened there in the years since it had been built, or possibly if some other house or building with tragic echoes had stood there before Cyrus Prescott laid the foundation for his family home. All of which was the only way either of them could imagine to figure out where the ghost had come from, and why.

And despite the morning's scare, Charlie couldn't picture anything she'd rather be doing less than this.

But she could picture a lot of things she would rather be doing. In great detail, in fact. Greater detail than she'd ever imagined before meeting Sam. Hot, sweaty, naked, intimate things . . .

"Charlie!"

Her head snapped up when Sam barked at her, and she shot him a glare that was half guilt and half embarrassment. "What?"

"Pay attention," he warned her, gesturing at the forgotten book. He'd closed the lid of his laptop and leaned forward, elbows on the table. He had such gorgeous hands, she thought as he steepled his fingers together, thoughtful for a moment. Long fingers, warm skin stretched taut over the knuckles, nicely shaped nails. She knew what those hands felt like against her skin, tangled in her hair, stroking the curve of her cheek. "At least tell me if you've found anything," he added, and she tore her gaze away from his hands.

She raised an eyebrow and pushed her glasses up on her nose. "I can tell you a dozen different uses for whale oil, the first warning signs of scurvy, ten different slang terms for the crow's nest, and general springtime wind patterns along the eastern seaboard. In other words, no."

"Perfect." He grunted and sat back. "I've got nothing, too."

"You know, I do have some information at the house," she said, frowning. "There's a family Bible and some scrapbooks, at least. I'm sure there's more, although I'd probably have to dig it out of the attic."

"No." He stood up, shaking his head. "We're not going back there."

She made an inarticulate noise, pure disbelief. "Sam, I live there. I have to go back eventually, you know."

He scowled at her and ran a hand over his head again. "I know that. But we're not going back there, not right now. Not . . . yet."

"Sam." She closed *The History of Whaling on Martha's Vineyard*—the title was as uninspired as the text, which was hardly a surprise—and folded her arms on it. "What happened this morning spooked me, I admit it. Especially after last night. That cold air and that sound . . ." She trailed off, trying to disguise her shudder with a roll of her shoulders. "But nothing's ever hurt me. And, well, I live there. I don't exactly have a choice about going back. Besides, there's Butch. He doesn't like changes."

He huffed out a breath and stood up, face set in hard, unforgiving lines. It was impossible to tell what he was thinking beyond the obvious grim determination in his expression—he believed in the ghost now, she knew that, but she was pretty sure he wasn't happy about it. Was he scared?

Unlikely, given his size and strength. Was he scared for her? Maybe. Was he scared of what happened whenever they were alone in that house together? Hell, she hoped not.

She didn't know him well enough to guess, and that was sobering. Because two hours ago she'd been ready to tear his clothes off and know him in a whole other sense. Somehow, she supposed, she should feel a little funny about that, but instead she felt funny that she didn't.

"Yeah, well," he said, oblivious to the confusion she was sure was clear on his face, and stuffed his laptop into the leather bag he carried it in. "You don't have to go back right now. Right now I think we should get some lunch. What do you say? You hungry?"

She stood up gratefully, and realized the English muffin she'd eaten at seven-thirty this morning was a distant memory. "I'm starved. And I know the best place on the island for French dip sandwiches."

"You should go back to the hotel and work on your article," Charlie told Sam after they'd eaten. They were standing on the front steps of the house, and Sam had taken hold of her hand as tightly as if she was about to jump off a cliff. "I'll be fine," she added gently, smiling at him. "I'm fed, I'm not spooked anymore, and I'm sure the fire department would be happy to battle ghosts if I called them."

"With what? High pressure hoses? Axes?" Sam asked. He stroked the back of her hand with his thumb again. God, what was it about that simple contact that went straight to her blood? "And I have plenty of time to work on the article, believe me."

"Well, I don't need a babysitter," Charlie insisted, and managed to extricate her hand from his, groaning at the way Sam growled in protest.

This was absurd. She didn't even know this man, and after one day she was melting with lust for him. She hadn't written anything worth a damn since yesterday morning, and suddenly she was more interested in the vaguely threatening ghost in her house and the definitely tempting man by her side than the novel she had been trying to write for seven years.

She had to get it together. Had to concentrate, focus, forget about Sam, if not the spirit upstairs, because at some point Sam would be gone, even if the ghost wouldn't be. She didn't need this distraction.

And part of her, a small, extremely shameful part of her, was confused about the fact that Sam wanted her at all.

She wasn't his type. She knew that much in her bones, even if she didn't know Sam very well. Sam was everything she wasn't—confident and traveled and even a little world-weary. He did everything fast, in that "get it done and get gone" way some men had. He wasn't right for her, a former English teacher who had had precisely four serious relationships in her life, and had never traveled farther west than New York City.

And given all of that, she couldn't understand why on earth he was interested.

But he was. He wrapped his arm around her waist as she looked at him, and she could feel the attraction in the way his body curved into hers, the heat in his eyes, and the gritty husk of his tone when he said, "I can work on the article inside, with you. Any objections?"

She had a million of them—sensible ones, even. Number one: letting herself fall for Sam was a risk of enormous proportions. But before she had a chance to think too hard, she heard herself saying, "Not at all. Come on in."

Chapter Eight

Their plan had worked for almost thirty minutes, Sam thought as he tugged Charlie's shirt off. He'd set up the laptop down in the kitchen with a re-heated cup of coffee and Charlie had gone upstairs to her office dutifully. They were going to work, they were going to be responsible adults, they were not going to discuss the supernatural or her family history, and they most definitely were not going to kiss. Or even touch.

Until ten minutes ago, when they'd collided on the staircase, Charlie coming down to ask him something pointless about Word's macro options and him going up to ask if he could pour himself another cup of coffee. At least they were both ter-rible liars, he thought, and tossed her shirt some-where behind him.

She whimpered a little bit, and reached for his belt buckle, but he wrestled her hands out of the way. "Not yet," he whispered, and felt a tug of heat in his groin when his words pulled another needy, desperate sound from her throat.

They'd stared at each other for all of five seconds on the stairs before he pulled her up against him and kissed her, licking hungrily into her mouth. Her arms had gone around him without hesitation, and when he'd steered her back up the stairs, she had taken the lead and pulled him into her bedroom.

The afternoon sun through the thin Roman shades at the windows bathed the room in gold light, a layer of warmth over the carpet and the gleaming wood; all Sam could see was bed and Charlie herself. She was trembling, blinking nervously, reaching for him in her old jeans and that loose white shirt, and somehow she was the most gorgeous, desirable thing he had ever seen.

They shouldn't do this, and he knew it. Not here, in this house. Not when he couldn't tell if the ghost or whatever otherworldly emanation it gave off was making them behave this way, which was so unbelievable he couldn't believe he was actually considering it. The problem was, he wanted Charlie too much to care, no matter what was making him feel that way.

But it wasn't right not to at least mention it, he argued with himself silently, pushing her backwards onto the bed gently. He'd stripped her down to her bra and panties in no time, both plain cream-colored satin, and he'd already lifted her glasses off and set them on the bedside table.

She caught his wrist in her hand, but he pulled

back quickly. "Charlie, we should talk," he managed, which was a definite accomplishment, given the pure need rushing hot in his blood. "This house, that heat . . ."

"I don't care," she said firmly and stood up, closing the few steps between them quickly. "I really, really don't."

"You're sure?" he said, and let her unbuckle his belt this time. Her fingers were surprisingly steady, and the minute the belt was unfastened, she unbuttoned his jeans and reached for the zipper. The polite thing to do was obviously to strip off his shirt.

"I'm so sure," she answered, her voice gone ragged and soft with desire. When she looked up at him, lips parted and still slick from their kisses, he gave in without a fight.

"I'm so glad," he whispered, stepping out of his jeans and black boxer briefs. He toed off his socks as she backed onto the bed, climbing up and kneeling on it until he came close enough for her to wind her arms around his neck.

"I want this," she said, mouthing along his jaw line. She was warm and soft against him, still vibrating with a fine ripple of excitement, and his cock was hard against her belly. "I know what I'm doing."

"I believe you," he said, voice gone rough with arousal as her fingers trailed over his shoulders and pecs, traveling down to learn the shape of his ribs. Her touch was light, wondering, the soft pads of her fingers just brushing the skin. "I want you, too, Charlie. So much."

He climbed onto the bed then and lowered her onto her back, kneeling over her and looking his fill. Her breasts were already flushed above the cups of her bra, and her hair had spilled out over the comforter in a golden brown fan.

Normally, he would take his time. Luxuriate in a new body to learn, tease and whisper and make it all easy and comfortable. Normally, he wasn't already hard enough to hammer nails and trying to remember his own name past the throbbing rush of blood in his head, in his belly. He could feel his own pulse skating higher as he simply looked at Charlie, and when she raised her arms, beckoning him closer, he knew there was no normal right now.

This was different. It was too urgent, too fierce, too undeniable. But normal or not, he was going with it, hell yeah.

Then he was stretched out over her, fitting their bodies together, and kissing her like she was the air he needed to breathe. She arched beneath him, rubbing her breasts against him, wrapping her legs around his waist, and he kissed her deeper, biting at her bottom lip and licking at her tongue, memorizing the taste of her.

"Want," she said faintly against his mouth, and wriggled beneath him. "Sam."

"What do you want, baby?" He mouthed along her collarbone, and swept his hand up her arm.

She was hot all over now, velvet skin flushed. "Tell me."

"Bra," she managed, pushing at his chest, and he kneeled up to reach around her and unhook it. It came away in his hands, loose scraps of silk, and he tossed it backwards, wincing when he heard a faint hiss.

"It's the cat," Charlie breathed, wriggling out of her panties laughing. "Ignore him."

"With pleasure," Sam answered, and slid down to take one rigid nipple in his mouth. They were both hard already, dark pink, straining away from the sweet white slopes of her breasts and begging for his mouth. He licked at the first one and stroked the second between his thumb and forefinger, thrusting his hips against her when she bucked up into the sensation.

"You like that?" he murmured, pulling at the nipple in his fingers until she shuddered, nodding. He answered by suckling her nipple deeper, using his tongue on the cushy underside to push it up against the roof of his mouth, drawing hard.

"Yes." The word was broken into at least three syllables, but he didn't even smile at the evidence of how desperate she sounded already, the way he usually would. He was right there with her—he'd been idling at ready since the porch, and he'd turned the corner, speeding into right now ten minutes ago.

He wanted to spread her open, lay her out and feast on her, pull those whimpering mewls out of her throat, but that was going to have to be later.

Much later, because right now he just wanted to be inside her, deep and hot and possibly forever.

Seventeen, he thought absently as he pressed kisses in the smooth valley between her breasts and stroked her hip. He'd been seventeen the last time he was this ready, this close to the edge before he'd even been inside.

Then it had been a senior girl, in his pal's narrow, slightly smelly bed while an end-of-summer party raged on outside the closed and locked door. He'd been hoping for weeks, putting his best effort into every make-out session, mentally calculating the number of times she'd let him go beneath her shirt, her bra, and finally into her panties with careful, shaking fingers.

When she'd showed him the condom she'd stolen from her older brother's dresser drawer after he'd brought her a dripping red plastic cup of beer from the keg Scott's older brother had provided, the rush of knowing he was about to lose his virginity had almost knocked him on his ass.

All told, he thought now, ignoring the way his cock twitched as he slid down Charlie's body, the friction sweet and hot against the swollen head, that first time had taken maybe three minutes. One finger inside her to see if she was wet, which his own older brother had told him was absolutely necessary, and then he'd rolled the condom on, fumbling with the slick latex and jerking a little at the snap when it was in place.

She'd gasped a little when he first thrust into her, and it wasn't like he'd imagined, it was strange and tight and unbearably exciting and . . . yeah, three minutes. Maybe.

That was a long time ago. He'd had a whole lot of fun since then. But something about Charlie put him back in that place of innocence. Well, this was his first time with her. He promised himself that it wasn't going to be the last.

And then she wrapped her legs around him, tightening them around his ribs and lifting her head to look down at him. "Sam," she breathed.

Twenty-five minutes at least, he thought a little wildly. He could definitely do that much.

Charlie didn't even know what she was asking for, really. Okay, well, that wasn't completely true, she wasn't a virgin, but this? She'd never wanted a man the way she wanted Sam right now.

And she didn't just want him, she needed him. At the moment, the long, solid weight of him on top of her felt like the only thing keeping her from breaking apart entirely.

She could feel him everywhere—the whispering sensuality of his breath on her skin, the wet, lazy swipe of his tongue, his fingers pressing into her hips, her waist, and, oh, sliding along her thigh now. The world had diminished to nothing but Sam and her own body, the sounds of their breathing as it husked out over skin, the gentle creak of the bedstead under the cushy mattress as they moved, the taste of his tongue in her mouth, the hot rush of blood pounding in her head.

"Sam," she said again, and spread her legs wider as he shouldered between them. His fingertips were tracing designs on her thighs as he kissed her belly and the delicate skin between her hipbones, and she still didn't know what she was asking unless it was more or now or please or all three.

"Let me taste you," Sam murmured, and she shivered, breath hitching in her throat. He slid even lower and slid one finger through the wet heat between her legs, careful, exploring, and then his mouth was there, pressing a soft kiss to the curls, mouthing at the folds, tongue licking into her.

Her head fell back on the pillows and she gasped out loud as her hips rocked up to meet him, knocking against his mouth.

"Easy, baby," he whispered, soothing her with a steady hand on her thigh. "Just a little more."

More? She could barely take this much, but it didn't matter, really, because she still wanted it, all of it, everything he could give her.

She'd never felt anything like this. She'd had sex, sure, and sometimes it had seemed pretty good. She loved kissing, even if she'd always been worried that she wasn't very good at it, and the "after" of sex, when it was over and it was all about lying in each other's arms, warm and loose and relaxed.

This wasn't relaxed. This was so far from relaxed, it was sort of terrifying, in fact, but it was also ridiculously good. She was beginning to understand why there were people who loved roller coasters and bungee jumping.

She was beginning to understand why people loved sex.

She knew, somewhere in the back of her head, where higher function was still possible, that she should think harder about this. About sleeping with a man she barely knew. About wanting to sleep with a man she barely knew so much that she could barely stand to wait another minute until he was inside her. About why she wanted him so much when she barely knew him, and why she had suddenly found this unexpected vein of courage running through her like ore through stone.

But that would have to come later, she decided as Sam licked into her again, tongue touching off a shower of sparks, fiery and hot, as he carefully circled her clit. So much later.

"Sam," she said again, and realized it was the only word left to her. She tried again, arching against his mouth at the same time, and came up with, "Please."

"Want to make you come first," Sam murmured once he'd pulled his mouth away. He kissed her thigh, lips wet against her skin, and then leaned down again.

She struggled onto her elbows, breathing shallowly as she watched him, his sandy head moving languidly as he kissed and licked her. The sight blazed through her like a flame—it was so intimate, so powerful, the way he was feasting on that dark, secret place—and before she could protest that orgasm didn't usually happen for her that way, or any way, he did something complicated and brilliant with his tongue.

Oh God, it was too much. She was coming, the

sensation rolling up from her toes, rough, sweet fire that lit her up from the inside out until she was gasping, shaking.

"Oh," she whispered when she came back to herself to find Sam crawling up her body again, kissing her all the way. "I . . ." There were no words for what that had felt like, how good it had been, but when Sam climbed off the bed entirely, she found her voice. "Um, Sam?"

He straightened up with a foil-wrapped condom in one hand, his eyes dark and intent. He ripped the package open as he stood by the bed, setting the wrapper on the bedside table. His erection was flushed dark with blood, and the tip was already shiny wet as it bobbed up against his belly.

"Oh," she said again, and bit her bottom lip. They weren't done. Yes. "Let me," she said, and held out her hand.

The mattress dipped when he climbed up again, kneeling over her. The rubber disc was slick and cool in her fingers, and she swallowed hard as she took his erection in her hand. There was a pulse on the underside, a heavy blue vein that ran the length, and the head was like a plum, flushed and ripe. A thready voice in her head whispered, Taste it, and she bent her head and did just that, without even thinking.

Sam groaned, a long, low, urgent sound, as she swirled her tongue around the head. It was salty and hot, and this close she could smell the dark musk of his skin. She'd never done this before with any man, not that there had been many—

one of them had been little more than a college boy, anyway—and she didn't know why.

A stupidly blissed-out part of her wondered if she'd simply been waiting for Sam.

"Charlie," Sam gritted out, as if it was his turn to communicate everything he wanted her to know by using simply her name.

She kissed the wet tip once more before angling up to roll the condom on, and then she fell back on the pillows. Sam didn't hesitate—he kneeled between her spread legs, using one finger in the folds of flesh to smear the slick wetness around her core. She bowed up, reaching for him, and he settled around her, driving home in one smooth thrust.

"Charlie," he whispered, and she found his mouth as she clung to his shoulders.

He felt so good inside her, filling her completely, the hot length of him sliding in and out as he rolled his hips. He sped ahead of her, thrusting hard at first, before a sudden, insistent side-to-side grind, and then all that hard heat bottomed out again before retreating, until she was nearly sobbing.

There was nothing but this, pleasure like a living thing inside her, twisting and traveling, clawing its way up and out, and she bit her lip hard as he thrust home again with a grunt. His face was so completely open, pleasure so naked and honest in his eyes, that the tension wrapped tight inside her uncoiled with a violent snap, and she came as he did.

For a moment they were both panting and shaking, frozen as the release shivered through them. Then Sam gently dropped his forehead to hers, and she wound her arms around his back. She'd been clinging to his shoulders so hard, she'd probably left bruises, she thought in a kind of wonder.

He kissed her, slow and easy, still buried inside her, and she waited for that moment she'd felt before, when it was simply comfortable, urgency faded to a warm, dull glow . . . and it didn't come. When he slipped out of her and rolled onto his back, dragging her up to his side with one firm arm, all she felt was an overwhelming loss, the need to have him inside her again as soon as possible, layered over the pleasure.

And that was frightening, really. As she laid her head on his chest, pushing up into the hand that stroked her hair steadily, she closed her eyes and felt the memory of that heat in the spare bedroom.

Desperate, punishing, consuming. And for the first time, she thought she understood where it had come from.

Chapter Nine

At six o'clock, Lillian couldn't stand it anymore. She'd been pacing around the shop all afternoon, Gloria at her heels, paging through invoices and Internet orders without really reading them, nodding at customers without making much conversation, her brain focused on the Prescott house and what Sam had told her was going on there.

Not all of what was going on there, of course. But she wasn't an idiot, and she could see the heat in Sam's eyes when he talked about Charlie.

That was . . . troubling. None of her business, either, but troubling nonetheless.

Not that she didn't trust Sam. She'd met more than her share of Sams in her lifetime, but she was willing to bet that Charlie hadn't. And even though most of the Sams Lillian had met were even less charming and nowhere near as smart as Sam Landry, not to mention as kind-hearted as she instinctively knew he was under that edgy exterior, she was willing to bet that Charlie was going to get thrown for a big fat loop, knocked on her delicate ass with her heart in her hands.

Men like Sam didn't stay put. Men like Sam didn't understand weddings and taking out the garbage and staggering out of bed in the middle of the night to soothe a baby with his mother's eyes and his father's healthy lungs. For a long time Lillian hadn't understood those things, either, or the desire for them, but Charlie was a romantic. Charlie had probably been dreaming about those very things since she was a kid. And, unless Lillian missed her guess, Charlie wasn't the type to give herself, body and soul, to a man when there was no hope that one day they might consolidate their dishes and CDs and argue over whose turn it was to do the dishes and put the CDs back in their cases, until they figured out they would be better off switching to paper plates and MP3s.

And then there was the issue of the ghosts.

Pages carried a skimpy selection of books on the paranormal, Lillian realized halfway through the afternoon, when her curiosity had gotten the better of her. It was tempting to rectify that but, then again, the store had never had much call for them before now.

Ghosts. It wasn't as if she'd never considered the idea before. Hell, she'd been through the Summer of Love and the subsequent years while still in grad school. She'd considered everything from raising her consciousness to the existence of alien life forms, free love, and the life-altering benefits of having your astrological chart done and eating more tofu. Ghosts seemed sort of tame in comparison, and living in New England all her life she'd heard more than her share of tales about things that went bump in the night.

And from what Sam had described, something was definitely going bump in the Prescott house.

She'd spent a frustrating hour on the Internet, trying to pick through amateur sites and complete nonsense until she found a few decent, basic descriptions of paranormal activity. Cold spots were a big red flag, but that had only happened once according to what Charlie had told Sam—whatever was going on in that house usually gave off heat.

In Lillian's mind, heat like that meant only one thing if it wasn't literal, and if there had been an enormous fire in the Prescott house, even way back, she would have heard about it.

Of course, it was a little surprising that she had never heard any of the Prescotts mention a ghost in the first place. She'd been living next door to the house since she was born, but the New England propensity for keeping skeletons, figurative or otherwise, firmly in the closet was more than familiar. It wasn't a trait she shared, but then she didn't come from ten generations of Bings. In fact, she was pretty sure that Bing had been her grandfather's alias when he'd left the Alps under a cloud for—stealing a cowbell? Decades later, she had no clear idea. Anyway, he'd had a hardscrabble life in upstate Vermont and some of his grown children had headed to the comparatively balmy climate of Massachusetts.

But the Prescotts—now, they went way back. And as far as what was happening with Charlie, either someone had unlocked the wrong door or the Prescotts were damn good at keeping secrets.

By six o'clock, she was pacing, irritable with frustrated curiosity, and stepping on Gloria every few feet she took. "That's it," she said, glaring down at the dog, which turned big, injured eyes up at her. "Time to go."

"I'm heading home," she told Jamie, tossing over the keys, and ignored her employee's sigh of relief.

She couldn't stop thinking about something supernatural in that house with Charlie. Whatever this was, it didn't sound like the harmless chains-rattling, tourist-pleasing kind of spook New Englanders loved. There was no way to know if whatever spirit had taken root in the house was actually dangerous, of course, but Sam's description of that growl didn't sound pleasant.

He was a writer, though, and he spun a good yarn. She hated that she was so easily drawn in, but it didn't really have as much to do with the possibility of a specter as it did with the fact that strange things were happening next door to her own house.

Even that wasn't entirely true, of course, she thought as she walked the few short blocks home, Gloria trotting beside her as usual, leashless and perfectly behaved, nails clicking on the sidewalk in the chilly winter evening. There were plenty of stories about ghosts just a stone's throw from here, right on the island, and they had never caused her more than a moment of passing curiosity.

But this ghost—what if it was a Prescott? The family didn't seem to deserve as many unhappy endings as she'd heard mentioned in whispers over the years.

She didn't usually dwell on what growing up next door to the Prescotts had meant to her—still meant, even now. Because that meant thinking about everything she was too afraid to fight for, once upon a time, when she was still too young to believe in things she couldn't see right in front of her face, concrete, or in black and white.

It was backwards and she knew it. Children were supposed to be the ones to believe in faeries, in Santa, in magic, and the power of wishes, but she was never that innocent, wide-eyed kind of little girl, something her mother had never failed to point out in exasperation. That kind of faith had come later—too late in her case, although knowing it didn't do her much good now.

When she rounded the corner onto Cottage Street, though, the idea of going home to the empty, echoing rooms of her own too-big house was too depressing to bear. There was more than one reason she was glad that Charlie had moved in, and one of the biggest was that she had become a friend to Lillian—despite the difference in their age and experience—in a way that Charlie's Aunt May never had.

Charlie's house wasn't any noisier than her own most of the time, but it seemed warmer with Charlie in it. And Charlie was always good for conversation and company, at least so far.

Besides, Lillian mused as she headed up the front walk to the Prescott house, Gloria following right behind her, she wanted to hear this ghost story from her.

And she wasn't above admitting that she really wanted to get a few details about Charlie's evening with Sam Landry. Hell, at her age she needed someone young and energetic to keep her amused with the occasional morning-after story or she was going to dry up completely.

Curious and shameless. *Story of my life,* she thought as she knocked at the front door.

No one answered, and the front hall and parlor were still dark. She walked the length of the porch, peering in the windows, and okay, she was a little ashamed of that, but not ashamed enough to keep her from going around the back. Especially when she spotted the faint glow of a light on in the kitchen, a pale yellow suggestion visible in the dining room.

Gloria pranced in front of her, stubby tail wagging, as she mounted the back porch steps. The dog jerked to a stop when Lillian did, because the back door window had no curtain, and she was fairly sure Charlie might have to rethink that in the near future.

Charlie was wearing Sam's shirt and apparently nothing else. Her bare legs were wrapped around Sam's waist as she sat on the counter, Sam in just his jeans as he stood between her legs, kissing her breathless, her head cradled in one of his big hands.

Lillian blushed for the first time in ages, blinking as she watched. Holy cow. It looked like they were going for the gold, right there on the kitchen counter. As if they were actually going to do it right there, both of them panting and flushed and completely unaware of anything that wasn't each other.

She wasn't that shameless, that was for sure. Cheeks burning, she turned and shooed Gloria along ahead of her, then nearly fell over her own feet in her hurry to get down the steps. Charlie might not have been prepared for a man like Sam, but she certainly seemed to be handling him with aplomb for the moment, Lillian thought with a return of her grin. The fallout could wait. And the ghost, or at least Lillian's curiosity about it, could definitely wait.

She had only gotten as far as the flagstone path to the driveway when she heard a brittle metallic crash, and then a scream. Charlie.

The echo of her own shriek still hovered in the room when the back door banged open. Lillian, Charlie thought absently, and gaped at her.

She was beginning to wonder if she was really awake. Lillian barging in unannounced was weird enough without the added fright of that cold blast of air and growling and the pushing that had backed Sam up against the opposite counter, rubbing the back of his hip where he had slammed into the butcher block.

"Lillian?" he said, voice stupidly thick, and Charlie slid down and crossed over to him while Lillian gathered Gloria in her arms, fingers stroking over the silky ginger ears as if the dog were the one that needed comfort.

"What the hell happened?" she demanded, taking a step closer. "I heard Charlie scream."

At least she was ignoring their relative lack of clothing, Charlie thought. That was something to be grateful for. Not that she really expected any different. Lillian was pretty hard to shock.

Sam just scrubbed a hand over his face and winced when Charlie prodded at his hip, insinuating her fingers into the loose waistband of his jeans. "Same thing that happened before," he said between gritted teeth. "That cold rush of air, and then I got shoved."

Lillian set Gloria down and came closer, her gaze focused on Sam's chest. Which was, Charlie realized with a fresh stab of horror, adorned with a red handprint. It was fading already, but its outline was still clear.

Charlie swallowed and went to the refrigerator, opening the freezer in search of a bag of frozen peas. This was crazy. The idea of a ghost was crazy enough, but a ghost that could leave a mark?

She turned Sam away from the counter and

held the bag to his hipbone. He winced, and turned dark blue eyes to her before attempting a ragged smile.

It was nothing like the smile she'd seen right before they'd fallen asleep, curled into each other, sweaty and sated, bodies like wet rags.

She swallowed hard, fighting the blush that threatened. If she closed her eyes, she could still feel him inside her, a heavy, perfect fullness. She'd dreamed about it while they slept, in fact, Sam inside her, Sam above her, the swollen, salty tip of his erection on her lips, and his mouth on her breasts, as if it was all happening again, or still.

They'd slept for nearly four hours, and the weirdest thing for Charlie was waking up with Sam's body curled protectively around her and feeling as if it was the most natural thing in the world. The room was shrouded in the dark gray shadows of late afternoon, but the bed and Sam's body were sleep-warm and soft around her, and even though it had been almost two years since she'd slept with a man, she was as comfortable waking up against his naked body as if they'd been together forever.

Lillian was inspecting the handprint on Sam's bare chest, and for once he was the one who was blushing, Charlie realized. That was sort of gratifying. She pulled his shirt down lower over her bare thighs, suddenly all too aware that it was the only thing she had on. God, Lillian was going to think she was a complete tramp. Then again, she didn't seem completely immune to the glorious sight of Sam's pecs and abs.

Maybe it was a good thing the ghost protested when it did, Charlie realized as she watched Sam wave away Lillian's concern. They'd come down hungry and half-dressed, and there was that strange non-weirdness again, as if she'd walked around half naked in front of Sam for years. As if sharing bits of cheese and an apple was something they were used to doing, as if letting Sam lick the tart juice off her fingers was the most natural thing in the world.

In her limited romantic experience, Guy #1 and Guy #2 never would have done that—it seemed hussyish to think of their names with Sam around, so she didn't. She'd dated Guy #3 for nine months and had never walked around naked in front of him, much less let him feed her from his hand and lick up and down the length of her body when she was only half-awake and drunk on the sensation, and that was a little overwhelming to think about.

Heck, she'd dated Guy #4 for over a year and it had never even occurred to her to feed him from her hand.

That's when the kissing had started again, of course. With the food and the mouths and the tongues. As if they hadn't just had the most incredible sex she'd ever experienced just a few hours ago. One more minute and Sam would have been inside her, right there on the kitchen counter.

She vaguely wondered if either one of them

would have noticed the ghost at that point, much less Lillian.

It was ridiculous to be thinking about this at all, when the topic at hand should have been why this spirit or whatever it was had taken such a vehement dislike to Sam. And why it had pushed him away from her in the attic and in the kitchen, but not when she and Sam had been in her bed, completely naked and having the kind of sex that made her leave a bite mark on his shoulder, which she had just noticed. Oops.

Lillian smacked her arm just hard enough to get her attention, and she jolted.

"Focus," Lillian said, and pulled out a chair at the kitchen table. "Sam told me about all of this today, so you don't have to worry that I think you're crazy. But I will admit that I never heard anything about a ghost in this house before, and that's a little weird, don't you think?"

Sam crossed his arms over his chest, but whatever self-consciousness he felt didn't stop him from questioning her. "Charlie told me you've lived next door all your life. Is that right?"

It was hard to pay attention when all Charlie could focus on was the way the muscles in Sam's back rippled when he tightened his arms. She tugged her shirt down farther over her legs and said faintly, "If you'll just excuse me for a second, I have to, um . . ."

"Yes, this could be a conversation that requires clothes," Lillian said not unkindly, despite the little smirk playing at one corner of her mouth.

"And food," Sam said suddenly, standing up. "Is there some place to order Chinese? I'm pizza'ed out this week already."

Grateful for the distraction, Charlie pulled take-out menus from the drawer next to the stove and handed them over. "Hong Kong Pearl is wonderful. I'd like chicken lo mein and pork dumplings. Oh, and two egg rolls." She thought for a minute. "And shrimp toast."

"Hungry, are you?" Lillian said, earrings winking in the glow of the lamp hanging over the table.

"Yes," Charlie said primly and fled upstairs with Sam's rumble of laughter echoing behind her.

This wasn't exactly what Sam had envisioned when he woke up wrapped around Charlie, he thought as he went upstairs and took his shirt back after calling in the Chinese food. Charlie was in the bathroom, and she'd left his shirt folded neatly on the thrashed bed, which struck him as sort of adorable.

No, what they'd started in the kitchen was much more like what he'd had in mind. Until the goddamned ghost had shown up and put a stop to it, anyway.

He shuddered a little, thinking about it. His arms full of Charlie and his tongue buried in her mouth, that cold blast of air had hit like a cartoon anvil, knocking the wind out of him even before the thing had shoved him five feet and slammed him into the counter.

That was the strangest part. That palm, as real and as solid as his own, or at least it felt that way when it connected with his bare chest, icy and relentless. Ghosts were supposed to be transparent, gauzy and insubstantial. Not shoving you around like a randy guy in a bar picking a fight over some girl.

Although Charlie was not, and never would be, just some girl to him.

He was halfway down the stairs when the doorbell rang, and Charlie came running down behind him.

"God, that was quick," she said, cheeks still pink and warm, her wallet in her hand.

"Must be a slow night in Edgartown for everyone who doesn't have a paranormal visitor." Sam grinned at her and looped an arm around her shoulder as he opened the door.

"That'll be $27.65," a kid with bored eyes and a nose like a ski slope said, holding up a heavy brown bag.

Sam pushed Charlie's hands aside and pulled his own wallet from his back pocket. "I've got this," he said softly, and kissed her forehead. "You can make me breakfast in the morning because I'm staying, no arguments."

Judging by the pleased smile that had filled out her mouth, she hadn't even been planning to try.

"Wow, that smells good," Lillian said. She'd already set out plates and silverware, and looked over her shoulder to ask, "Where are the napkins, honey?"

"Cabinet beside the fridge," Charlie said and took carton after carton from the bag. There was a big greasy smear on the bottom, and Sam ripped a paper towel from the roll on the counter and set it down on the table under the bag. He was absurdly pleased when she turned a grateful smile on him.

They spread out the food and sat down, and Sam speared up a piece of beef before he launched into his theories.

"So ghosts usually are all about unfinished business," he said, and paused to take a bite. "That's the prevailing wisdom anyway, and it makes sense."

"Do you think the season has something to do with its bad mood?" Lillian asked thoughtfully. "Maybe the emanation just hates shopping."

"Or maybe the ghost always wanted to make her own Christmas cards but never got around to it and sent out storebought ones instead. Do you mean that kind of unfinished business?" Charlie asked Sam wryly.

"No. Guilt never happens to the right people. Now if it was someone who snowed their friends and family with preprinted Christmas letters that arrived postage due, then definitely, the ghost should feel guilty." He laughed.

Lillian finished up a mouthful of fried rice. "What makes you think it's a her?" she said to Charlie.

Sam shrugged. "Because women obsess over Christmas in a way that men don't."

"I thought it was a her," Charlie said softly. She was examining the egg roll in her fingers as if it held the answers. "I still do, sort of. Except the thing that pushed Sam doesn't seem like a woman, does it? Maybe we need to get a ghost count."

Sam held up two fingers. "I would say more than one and less than three."

Charlie nodded. "Sounds reasonable."

"If there is anything reasonable about this." Sam sat up straighter. "Anyway, one of them is male. I don't know a lot of women who can push that hard." He held up a hand when Lillian started to protest. "Gloria Steinem notwithstanding."

She rolled her eyes, and reached down to offer Gloria a bit of her sesame chicken. The dog scarfed it up happily and panted for more, thin tail banging against Sam's calf.

"Yes, well, whatever gender our ghost or ghosts are, they are agitated, that's for sure," Lillian said. "They don't seem to be the nice, polite, drift-around kind at all." She stared across the table at Charlie, brow creasing into a frown. She managed to look both maternal and fierce, and Sam swallowed a smile with his next bite of beef and broccoli. "I don't like the idea of Charlie being here on her own with some pushy ghost who has anger management issues."

"She's not going to be on her own," Sam said before Charlie could get a word in, but he didn't miss the doubt and concern on her face. "I'm not going to let anything happen to her. And anyway, whatever this thing is, it only seems to be pissed off at me."

"Sam." Charlie's tone was harsher than he expected, and even Lillian was startled, but her mouth was filled with fried rice. "Reality check." Charlie pointed her chopstick at him. "You have the article to finish." Behind her glasses, her eyes were wide, searching. "You haven't told me your itinerary, but it's not like you're going to be hanging around Martha's Vineyard for months."

"Um—"

"And Christmas is coming, much as all of us would like it to get itself over with so it will be January sooner. Am I making myself clear?"

"Sort of," Lillian mumbled.

"What I'm saying, Sam, is that you'll be leaving soon to be with your family—or someone. But not staying here any longer than you have to."

It wasn't really a question, and the silence in the room was broken by the cat batting a stray chow mein noodle across the floor until Gloria barked and Butch hissed at her.

Lillian was staring daggers at him, but he ignored her to slide a hand across Charlie's on the table. "No, I don't think so."

She squeaked out a barely audible why-not that made him smile. Had he ever seen such eagerness in a woman's eyes?

"Charlie, you're right about the deadline, and I have to do some more interviews, but I could use the island as home base while I work. I'd like to, anyway."

It was true, all of it, even if it was as surprising as finding a real haunt. And when Charlie's face softened, it was all the encouragement he needed.

Chapter Ten

The book was back in her mind—the second book, the naughty one—and the hero and heroine were being as bad as they wanted to be. Charlie chalked it up to the snow, which had arrived last night, iced up the windowpanes. It was pretty to look at from inside, she decided. She'd seen Lillian out walking her dachshund. Gloria's thick cylinder of a body was bundled up in an adorable candy-cane striped sweater and the dog was leaning into the wind, her soulful eyes squinted nearly shut.

The older woman called a hello to the retiree with the ancient golden retriever, which watched from the window as its master attempted to pùt chains on his tires.

"Isn't winter in New England wonderful?" Lillian screamed into the biting wind. The old man didn't seem to hear. The Red Sox cap had been replaced by an earflappy thing lined with bunny fur.

Charlie went upstairs to look for her writing notes and found them, but she didn't have to read them. As before, the scene played out as if she were seeing it scroll by on a monitor while she wrote them.

"Again," Temperance whispered, and smoothed her hands over Daniel's back. His skin was flushed hot. Smoothly, the muscles beneath it rippled like water, fluid as a wave curling in on itself as it returned to shore. If she lived to be a hundred, a thousand, she would never get enough of him like this, naked and strong and arching under her hands.

He groaned as he drove into her once more, harder now, unforgiving, the head of him touching home until she clenched around him, holding him there. He hated this, when she made him wait, demanded that he thrust only at her command.

"Shhh," she soothed him, trailing her lips along his cheek, the salty slick edge of his jaw. Daniel was not a patient man, not when he was buried in the slippery darkness between her thighs.

She tightened around him again, tilting her hips, and let an incoherent sound of her own escape her throat. He filled her completely, hard and hot and pulsing in that secret place inside her, a glorious weight above her. When she moved, the tip of him touched off a singing spark of pleasure, and she ground against him again, seeking more.

"Let me, love," he panted against her neck,

breath hot and damp. His arms trembled with effort as he braced above her. "Let me now, please."

"Not yet," she breathed. Digging her heels into the firm flesh of his behind, she held him close. A sultry breeze fluttered the curtains at the window, full of sea salt and pine, and a carriage rolled by outside, wheels heavy on the road, the clopping hooves of the horses marching in lazy time. "Wait, Danny. Please."

He growled at her, biting into the slope of her shoulder, not quite gently. She hissed and rocked her hips up, whispering, "Now."

Without hesitating, he withdrew, a slow, burning slide, and then drove home again, pushing the breath out of her in a ragged gasp. Again and again he thrust now, shaking with the need to let go, to let the pleasure come, and she hung on, fingernails scoring crescent moons into his shoulders. There was no stopping him now, and she loved the wild snap of his hips against her, the full, thick length of him sliding into her wetness, the hitch in his breath before it washed over him and he stiffened above her.

When he finally pulsed inside her in a hot, wet rush, he always breathed her name as if it was the only word he could remember, the only thing that mattered, before he collapsed on top of her, pressing heated kisses to her cheeks, her shoulders, her forehead.

And every time, it was then that she shattered,

breaking apart beneath him with his name on her lips.

Well, she felt warmer now, she thought, looking at the window. The frost crystals on it had crept higher.

"Just a little more, baby," Sam breathed, and Charlie shuddered as he drove deeper inside of her.

He was spooned up behind her, both of them still nestled in the rumpled warmth of the sheet and comforter, one hand curved possessively around her breast as he thrust further inside her. It was almost too much in this position, but she didn't want him to stop. She never wanted him to stop.

And that scared her. This wasn't her, this wasn't any version of herself she'd ever come close to imagining. The Charlie Prescott she'd always been only had sex after a series of regulation dates, and then usually in a bed, not—nearly anyway—on the kitchen table or counter.

Or tangled on the sofa in the front of the fireplace, the way they had last night when the oncoming snowstorm had begun to howl. Sam had suggested the fire, but Charlie was the one who found herself climbing into Sam's lap as the flames licked fast and hot at the dry kindling, casting a dull red-orange glow over the front parlor.

She groaned as Sam drove deep again, his

fingers stroking her nipple and then lower, skating across her belly and down, soothing the taut muscle as it went.

"Is that good?" Sam whispered, taking her earlobe between his teeth before she could answer. She whimpered in response as his hips rolled up, the low grit of his voice drawing a shiver out of her. "You like me inside you?"

"Yes," she breathed, and twined her fingers with his as he reached lower still, brushing the curls gently.

Like was such a useless word, she thought a little wildly as he guided their fingers between the slick folds and circled the wet skin where they were joined. Like didn't even begin to cover it.

But even so, she was pretty sure that the man wrapped around her wasn't the Sam he usually was, either. She was a little bit ashamed at how little she knew about him, but it wasn't a stretch to believe that Sam Landry was the love 'em and leave 'em, one-night-stand kind of guy.

And yet here he was, still in her bed, and neither one of them could seem to stop touching the other. Last night they'd finally picked themselves up from the sofa and moved upstairs only to get in bed and reach for each other all over again.

But . . . that didn't feel exactly wrong, either.

Sam was still driving slow and steady inside her, in no rush, and she relaxed into the rhythm, letting him rock forward into her, spreading her legs a little to accommodate his fingers against her clit. She was so wet, open and pliant for him as pleasure beat like restless wings in her belly, and it was hard to remember that this would have to end at some point.

But it had to. She needed to work on the book, figure out what the heck was haunting her house before someone really got hurt, and he had an article to write and research to do, not to mention a whole life somewhere else she didn't know anything about. She didn't even know where he lived, for heaven's sake.

She was playing with fire, that was for sure. Sam was that hot. Each stroke touched off a new spark of pleasure, and she twisted her head to seek out his mouth. He was waiting for her, lowering his head to hers and claiming her mouth in a slow, wet kiss that went on and on as he pumped inside her, faster now.

There was so much she didn't know. She'd tried to ask a few semi-intelligent questions last night, and he'd silenced her line of inquiry with kisses and urgent, exploring passes of his hands.

He arched his back, snapping his hips up deeper, harder, and she closed her eyes, all thought driven out of her head for the moment. There was only this, the heated connection between their bodies, the sensual thump of his hips against her behind and his erection sliding home again and again, and they came within minutes of each other, Sam grunting out a choked warning and Charlie sobbing out an inarticulate noise as she bowed around

him, orgasm bubbling up from somewhere deep
and rushing through her like water.

"So good," Sam breathed a moment later, and
took his hand from between her legs. When he
slid the fingers that had stroked her into his
mouth, a tremor of fresh arousal rippled through
her, and she tightened around him, where he was
still buried inside.

It was better than good. Charlie didn't think
there was a word for what was between them.
But she did know she didn't ever want it to end.

"Toast's up," Sam said, grabbing the browned
slices of bread and tossing them on a plate. Charlie was pouring juice, and the scent of freshly
brewed coffee and buttery fried eggs and crispy
bacon hovered in the kitchen.

"You can start," Charlie said over her shoulder
as she put the carton of OJ back in the fridge.
Dressed in a plain gray robe and little else, her
hair scooped into a loose ponytail on the back of
her neck, she was still the sexiest, loveliest thing
Sam had ever seen. "Just put in two pieces for me
before you do?"

He kissed the back of her neck when he started
her toast, letting his tongue linger over a warm
purple mark in the shape of his teeth. She melted
back against him, purring low in her throat, and
his groin tightened in response.

Yikes. He had to learn to keep his distance for

at least a few minutes at a time or they were never going to get out of this house.

He pinched her rear end lightly before he sat down at the table and picked up his fork, grinning at her startled gasp. She grabbed her toast and set it on her plate just as he was biting into the first piece of his bacon, dripping with runny golden yolk.

"So I'm thinking I'll hit up the historical society today and look into the Prescotts," he said when she was seated across from him, salting her eggs carefully. "I'd really like to get up to Boston, because there's a group of paranormal experts, or so they call themselves, up there."

She looked up, startled, her brows drawn together and making a worried dent in her forehead. His thumb itched to reach out and smooth it away. "Paranormal experts?"

"As expert as they get, I guess," he said, and slopped up more yolk with the crust of his toast. "A friend of mine wrote a piece on them a few years back, and he was pretty impressed. Maybe they could help us figure out how this ghost happened into existence, and how to get it the hell out of this house."

"Sam."

He glanced up, toast halfway to his mouth, and frowned at her obvious unhappiness.

"Why . . ." She sighed heavily, and pushed her plate away. "Why bother? It's not hurting anyone."

"Uh, I beg to differ," he told her, and arched an eyebrow.

"Okay, aside from that whole pushing thing, which I'll admit isn't exactly friendly, but . . ." She licked her lips nervously and fixed her eyes on him before continuing. "That's only about you, so far, and . . ."

He waited, but she seemed to have stalled, hands folded in her lap and her eggs congealing on her plate.

"And?" he prodded, driven to ask by emotions he wasn't ready to name. The sunlit kitchen was too quiet suddenly, even if the air was charged with unspoken words.

"I don't know," she said finally, and it was hardly more than a whisper. "I don't know what I mean. I'm just tired, I think."

And he wasn't going to be around forever. Those were the words she'd locked down tight, and he knew it. He set down his toast and pushed away from the table, taking his mug to the counter under the pretense of pouring himself more coffee.

She wasn't wrong, of course. He didn't live here. He wasn't looking for whatever this was and never mind his gallantry in front of Lillian. This was turning into a . . . a relationship. And he'd known it that first night he'd kissed her, known that he shouldn't have done it, that Charlie wasn't the type to throw herself into a fling just for the sake of some good sex and a little easy company.

And now? He couldn't get more than five feet away from her without feeling the need to touch her, to remind himself of the giving heat of her body, the taste of her mouth.

Which was strange, to say the least. It wasn't like him to be emotional, to want someone that much. Hadn't been, for more years now than he could count, and he was okay with that. More than okay, in fact.

But it didn't stop the tug of guilt when he turned around to find her staring stubbornly at her plate.

"I don't want you to get hurt," he said softly, and walked up behind her, skimming his fingers over her shoulder, down the graceful slope of her head, her hair soft and warm under his hand.

"I don't think the ghost is going to hurt me," she said, and he nodded even though she couldn't see it.

He didn't think whatever was going on in this house was going to hurt her, either. He was. They just weren't talking about it.

She wasn't snooping, Lillian told herself as she folded her napkin in her lap at lunch that afternoon. Snooping was an old-ladyish thing to do, and while she might be over sixty, she firmly believed that she was not old and never would be.

What she was doing was caring. Looking for information that might help Charlie figure what or who was haunting that big old house she'd inherited. Nothing at all wrong with that, was there?

Funny how it had still felt wrong when she'd called Iris Munson this morning, after months had passed since they'd seen each other, and asking her to lunch. At Iris's favorite restaurant, no less, The Crow's Nest.

It was almost reassuring to finally know how shameless she was, underneath it all.

"I'm thinking of the chowder," Iris said now, happy and relaxed as she perused the menu. "Of course, I always get the chowder when I come here, but it really is the best, don't you think?"

Lillian managed an agreeable smile in answer. She'd known Iris since they were both girls, far younger than Charlie was now, and even though Iris's artsy-craftsy, earth mother vibe had grated as far back as high school, Lillian had never been able to resist her friend's honest affection. Iris doted on Lillian and, despite her many quirks, Iris had a heart as big as Nantucket Sound and a memory as long as the centuries-old turnpike that crossed Massachusetts. If anyone knew something about the Prescotts, it would be Iris.

"What are you getting, dear?" Iris asked as she folded her menu. "And to what do I owe the pleasure of your company today?" She beamed from beneath the wire-framed glasses she'd started

wearing in the last few years. They were as red as
her hair, and her lipstick, Lillian noticed. "I may
be a grandmother, but it doesn't mean I have to
neglect my looks," she'd told Lillian two years
ago. Lillian's cropped pewter hair was an affront
to womanhood, in Iris's opinion.

"It's been too long, that's all," Lillian told her,
pushing down a stab of guilt at the fib. The waitress was approaching, and Lillian smiled in her
direction. The sooner they ordered and she could
get Iris on the right track, conversationally, the
sooner she could get out of here. "I thought it
was time we caught up."

"Well, I'm glad you did." Iris squeezed her hand
across the table. "I brought pictures of Annabel
and Lindsay, too."

Oh good, Lillian thought dispiritedly as her
friend ordered. Beaucoup de grandchildren with
tiny-toothed smiles. More fibbing about how
cute they were.

When she'd ordered a lobster roll and a cup of
coffee, she sat back in her chair and stared out the
window at the Sound. The snow hadn't melted and
its brightness was dazzling to look at. Shining
on it, the sun's reflection threw diamonds over the
rippling water. The postcard-perfect Christmas-is-
coming weather and the wreaths and garlands on
the houses along the street added up to blinding
reality of the happiest sort. It was hard to believe
that Charlie had a home-for-the-holidays ghost or

ghosts who were quite unpredictable. Of course, that was the nature of apparitions.

But Lillian had seen that angry red handprint on Sam's chest. She'd heard Charlie scream. The ghostly visitors had announced themselves several times over but belief didn't make it any easier to pinpoint their identity. The Prescotts hadn't been the happiest family in the world, certainly, but even after living next door to them for more than sixty years, Lillian couldn't imagine who among them would come back to haunt the living.

But Iris oughta know. She had been a historical society docent for almost twenty years now, and she had taken it upon herself to research the island's seagoing families. A book, privately printed, was planned. Lillian would have to stock it whether she wanted to or not. It would sell a few copies in the summer months.

She murmured appropriate praise when her friend passed a parade of snapshots under her nose: Annabel in her pajamas, Lindsay with a glittery tiara on and a pink tutu riding slantways on one tiny hip over her jeans.

"Grandchildren really are such a joy," Iris said, her voice softening mawkishly, and Lillian braced herself.

"And I'm not going to have any," Lillian told her a little more firmly than was probably necessary. "That's all right with me, and you know it, so you don't need to get all wet about it every time we see each other."

Iris blinked at her, mildly insulted as usual, but in the end she simply pushed her glasses up her nose and sat back. "What's it like to have Charlie living next door now? Does it bother you?"

It was Lillian's turn to blink. "Where on earth did that come from?"

The waitress passed by with a tray for the table next to them, and Iris leaned in to lower her voice. "Oh, Lillian, don't be dense. It must be a little difficult for you to have her living there, right next door. I've met her, you know. She looks awfully like her father."

Fists. She was making fists under the table, but as long as she didn't use them, it was all right, Lillian assured herself. "Iris, we've talked about this a million times . . ."

"I know it," Iris retorted, and beamed up at the waitress, who was taking her chowder from a tray. "But that was before Michael's daughter moved in next door and you got chummy with her, so I think the topic deserves a bit of attention, don't you?"

Lillian gritted her teeth until the waitress had set her plate and coffee down, and then glared across the table at her friend. "All that is over and done with, I've told you that for years. The man is dead, for goodness' sake."

Iris opened her mouth, but Lillian glared harder. "As for Charlie, she's a lovely young woman I would be happy to know no matter who she was,"

Lillian went on, distressed to realize she was actually wagging her finger. "So . . . there."

She scowled when Iris lifted an eyebrow, amusement plain on her face. "Fine. Let's drop the subject then. Instead why don't you tell me, honestly now, why you wanted to have lunch. Usually I have to put my foot down and demand it, and you know it as well as I do. I'm not as absentminded as I look, dear." She picked up her iced tea glass and shook it lightly, the ice cubes tinkling musically. "So what is it you need?"

One day, Lillian decided, she was going to make a note to remind herself that Iris was not, in fact, as ditzy as she liked to appear. She let her shoulders sag, knowing she was in for some smug crowing from her friend when she said, "I need you to tell me everything you know about the Prescott family."

Chapter Eleven

"Stop it, Butch," Charlie warned the cat sometime around two o'clock. He'd jumped on the desk for the third time, and was attempting to curl up on the computer keyboard, which was simply weird as well as annoying. Of course, she couldn't really blame him for assuming the space was up for grabs—she hadn't written a word since she sat down. And it was one of the warmer spots in the house. The old glass in the windowpanes shook, buffeted by the wind, which had begun to blow again, picking up the drifted snow in little swirls.

This was ridiculous. She stared into her mug of cold coffee before standing up to roll her neck and shoulders. Maybe a change of scene would do the trick, get her brain moving again. Caffeine certainly hadn't worked.

She carried the mug downstairs, Butch padding behind her on the smooth wooden treads. Maybe this was what always happened when you plunged into a steamy fling, she thought as she dumped out the contents of her mug and rinsed it in the sink. She hadn't been able to think straight for, what, days now, and she certainly hadn't slept very well.

Not that the kind of not-sleeping she'd been doing was anything to complain about. She bit her lip as she stood leaning against the counter, the rushing water from the faucet forgotten as she tried to suppress a grin.

She could spend a few more days—heck, a few weeks—mapping Sam's body. Straight through Christmas and into New Year's Eve, which was, after all, the ultimate couples holiday. New Year's Day . . . that they could devote to champagne detox with aspirin and tea and long naps in each other's arms.

Yeah. He could rock her for days.

Exploration was a pleasure she'd never considered before—a man's body was interesting in its own way, and the ones she'd known had been attractive, but Sam was different somehow.

Sam let her explore, for one thing. Sam didn't need to rush, wasn't focused on the moment he could be inside her, not that he objected to it, of course. He was perfectly willing to lie back and let her touch him, press her mouth to him there and there and then there, tasting the subtle differences between hipbone and shoulder, testing the weight of bicep as compared to thigh. She'd already fallen in love with the shallow dent at the base of his spine, the coffee-colored birthmark that rode high on one shoulder, the wrist bones that seemed just knobby enough for hands as strong as his were.

It was a bit like unlocking him, piece by piece, she thought, and jumped when the cat landed on the counter beside her to swat at the water still gushing from the tap. She shut it off and set Butch down on the floor before she wandered out of the kitchen and came to a stop before the window in the front parlor.

Unlocking Sam's heart might take a little longer than his body, she realized as she stared out at the December day. She was getting an idea by now of how generous Sam could be, how tender as well as how interestingly fierce, how intelligent he was and how irreverently funny, but she didn't know what any of it meant.

At the moment, she wasn't even sure she wanted to find out. She just wanted him to come back later this afternoon, so she could kiss him, and stroke her hands down his heaving rib cage as he thrust into her.

She blushed just thinking about it. Desire was a powerful thing when it hit this hard, and she was still a little surprised that the sheer intensity of it hadn't knocked her flat.

Butch wound around her ankles, tail flicking lazily, and she roused herself out of her thoughts. That was part of the heat she'd felt up in the spare room—intensity. Passion so overwhelming and powerful it had blazed right through the years, even when—she was guessing but she sensed that it was a good guess—life itself had gone.

But whatever had pushed Sam away from her was no less intense. Somehow the two things had to be related—as absurd as the existence of one spirit seemed, two random, completely different ghosts were even farther out of the realm of possibility.

Marshaling her determination, she grabbed Butch and headed upstairs. If she couldn't write, she was going to sit up in that room and wait for the ghost to come back.

Sam flipped his cell phone shut and threw it on the bed beside him before he flopped on his back. Bridget Hartigan of Narragansett, Rhode Island, was expecting him two days from now, to discuss the weeping woman who had been haunting the attic of the Seaswept Inn for the past hundred years.

He didn't have a choice about going. Kevin had left no less than eight separate voice mails and six e-mails in the last two days, demanding Sam get in touch and asking for updates about the article.

"Dude, you're new here, you know," he'd said in the last voice mail, sent just this morning. His tone had been silky, sure of himself, and Sam had tightened his jaw so hard while listening it still ached vaguely. "Maybe you were hot stuff wherever you worked before, but you're working for *Scoop* now. For me. Not happy with that? Things can change, you know. Fast."

Well, Sam would have been happy if *Scoop* printed its last issue and then went up in flames, metaphorically speaking. It was a gossip rag, nothing more than recycled celeb sightings and teen stars' favorite ice cream flavors, with the occasional sensational human interest piece readers apparently couldn't get enough of. Sam hated it the way he hated pistachios and unexplained traffic jams and the Yankees' new manager.

But he'd made his bed, as the saying went, and now he had to lie in it. Plus the economy was not going to come out of its nosedive any time soon. He chided himself for mixing metaphors. At least, he thought, sitting up and staring at his meticulously kept hotel room, he got to lie down in said metaphorical bed with Charlie now and then.

For the time being, anyway.

First he had to tell her he was heading to Rhode Island, and then up to Gloucester, where the story went that an eerie voice had been heard in the basement, and strange liquid had been oozing from between the ancient bricks.

If he had to include the word "ectoplasm" in this article, he was going to buy the biggest bottle of scotch he could find and dive in headfirst.

He rolled off the bed and stood up, easing the kinks out of his shoulders. The desk in the room was a tiny, delicate thing made almost entirely of gingerbread trim as far as he could tell, but working on the bed wasn't exactly a better option. Working at Charlie's kitchen table would have been more sensible, and much more comfortable, and for a minute he wondered what on earth had convinced him to come back to the inn this morning instead.

Then he remembered the way Charlie had looked in her robe, still sleep-soft around the edges, hair tousled and cheeks pink, and he grunted. Yeah, working at Charlie's would have meant taking her back to bed, or possibly just taking her right there in the kitchen.

It wasn't an entirely comfortable thought, either. He'd been with enough women to know what infatuation was, what good old lust was, the way a hot hookup flamed to life and then fizzled out, and what he and Charlie had between them was somehow nothing like any of that. It was explosive, it was demanding, it was like a goddamn force of nature.

He didn't get it, that was the thing. And what was worse was the high probability that he was going to hurt her without wanting to, just because this couldn't last. Good things didn't. And he was going to cut out right around or just after Christmas, which was generally not the most wonderful time of the year, no matter how that damn song went.

That had been clear enough this morning.

Charlie Prescott was smart and big-hearted and brave and sweet and adorable but, despite all that, he wasn't the right guy for her. He wasn't sure who would be, really, and automatically hated all the other potential candidates for this lifetime and the next. Whatever. None of the women he dated—

okay, sometimes simply slept with—had wanted the things he knew Charlie would want eventually. Marriage, kids, asking him to take out the garbage while she finished loading the dishwasher, anniversary dinners with house wine, and sitting together at school plays and PTA meetings.

He shook his head as he leaned over to power off his laptop. It wasn't a bad dream, he guessed, if you were into that, but no one was going to convince him it ever worked the way it was supposed to. People said a lot of things—"I love you" and "It's forever" and "Trust me"—but it didn't make them true. It didn't make them mean any more than the air it took to speak them aloud.

No, Sam liked facts. And right now the only fact that interested him was how much he wanted Charlie. Wanted her, not loved her. He didn't even lie to himself.

And as long as she wanted him, he was going to be there. There, he thought suddenly, glancing out the window, in her house, if she would have him.

He tossed his dirty clothes into one side of his suitcase, patting down the clean, folded stuff to make it all fit, and grabbed up his cell phone and laptop. Parka hood up and half-blinded by the fur trim, he slid his key across the counter to the bored young guy downstairs at the front desk.

"I'm checking out," he said without thinking twice. "I'd like to settle my bill."

* * *

Butch had balked when Charlie had tried to carry him into the spare room, which she took as a hopeful sign despite the claws digging into her sweater as he tried to leap from her arms. If he was spooked, then it meant he'd sensed something, or at least that's what everyone said about pets and the supernatural. So she'd soothed him with a few long, gentle strokes and the shushing noise that always made him purr, and he'd finally settled against her shoulder, even though his ears were pressed flat to his head.

He'd curled up against her when she climbed onto the bed, leaning back against the pillows with a deep breath. Nothing felt out of the ordinary to her yet, but then she'd never gotten any kind of warning. So she settled back, carefully cataloging everything she knew about this room.

She was pretty sure it had been her dad's room when he was growing up, long before it had been painted lavender. She'd noticed the name Michael Prescott carved in an inconspicuous place inside the closet, the way a kid staked a claim. He and her mom had stayed in here when they came to visit, with Charlie in the room she had turned into her office—her aunt May's girlhood room. The dear and departed, she thought. Not that the Prescotts had ever been all that warm or demonstrative as a rule. Of course, that could change, she thought with a wry smile, wishing Sam were here to distract her. She'd love to be the first passionate Prescott. And have a few little Prescotts to raise in happiness.

As if the overly long holiday season wasn't potentially depressing enough without thinking about being the last of the family line, she scolded herself. Maybe, just maybe, given the supernatural happenings, there was a curse on the house and she was next in line for something awful. Wait five more minutes and a Christmas zombie might pop out of the walls, shiny gift paper and curling ribbons in its cold, cold hands.

She laughed to herself, knowing she'd conjured that up out of her own ineptitude at wrapping presents. Come to think of it, she hadn't bought any. But there was, what, two or three weeks to go? She wriggled when Butch kneaded at her arm, shifting to scratch behind his ears. No need to think about things like that, not here, not now. She focused, concentrating on the room, and on what she could remember of it from growing up.

It had been a guest room almost as far back as she could recall. Robbie and Susannah, her cousins, had been given two rooms on the third floor once they were in middle school, and Charlie only vaguely recalled playing in here once when the room was still Susannah's, bright pink and frilled with white eyelet and lace. That visit, she was pretty sure her parents had been in Aunt Margaret's girlhood room, with Charlie in a sleeping bag right here on the floor.

Her Prescott cousins were still very much alive, but where they were, she had no idea. Scattered across the country. A brief look on Facebook hadn't turned up a thumbnail that looked like either one and that was about as far as she'd gotten.

She sighed, wishing she had more family going on than that. So what was with this room anyway? She had slept in it, Susannah and her father had grown up here, in different generations, and maybe one of them had felt what she had at some point. But no one had ever breathed a word of it if that were true.

Typical New Englanders. Afraid to let the neighbors know anything the least untoward was taking place in their proper family.

Why? Their sins had been small ones, as far as she knew. By current standards of human behavior, admittedly low, not sins at all.

Charlie had once caught Aunt May looking at the sleek contemporary furniture in the Sunday ads more than once, but would she buy any? Of course not. Such pieces weren't right for an old Victorian, even if she loathed every fussy little chair and scrap of chintz in the house. Aunt Margaret had always insisted on dress-up clothes and honest-to-God hats on Easter Sunday, because that's what was done. Questions about the more interesting things in life, like love and sex and what to do when a boy kissed you were met with polite non-answers from them and her parents.

And then there had been too many funerals for the usual routine reasons and no one left to even ask. She thought again that she ought to make more of an effort to find her cousins.

Somehow, timid as she'd been in her life, she

knew she wasn't very much like the rest of the Prescotts. Was she being visited, if that was the term, for that reason? She shook her head to clear it, wondering if she was more receptive to freaky phenomena.

She was certainly good at looking for trouble. Here she was, all alone, awaiting the arrival of a ghost that seemed to be made of pure emotion . . . and physical sensation . . . with no idea who or what it was . . .

She gasped when the first wave of heat hit her, a blast as potent as the icy air that had blown into the room the other night. She struggled to breathe through it, suffocating under the hot, thick pressure of it. It had never come this quickly before—it usually oozed in gradually so she would find herself slightly warm before realizing that the heat was so solid she could practically smack it with her hand.

But she couldn't panic, even though Butch had already begun, hissing and spitting as he slunk off the bed and streaked out of the room.

"Thanks, kitty," she muttered under her breath, her lips dry already in the blistering heat. "I'm getting a dog tomorrow. Serves you right."

She just needed to relax. That was all. If she simply tried to experience this, maybe she could sense something. Maybe she would be able to see or feel who was behind that formless sensuality that engulfed her.

Wiping a bead of sweat from her forehead, she closed her eyes, and tried to focus on breathing through the humid press of heat in her lungs. In and out, she breathed as carefully and slowly as she could, listening, waiting, wondering if she was trying too hard.

Wondering, too, if she was a little crazy after all.

Stop it, she admonished herself silently, blowing out another breath and registering the sheen of moisture on her cheeks and forehead. It was so hot, so stuffily close in the room already, she had to fight the urge to crawl off the bed and get away. That was what she had always done before, and she was never going to figure this out if she ran.

She took another deep breath, shifting on the comforter, and then froze.

Something, someone, was whispering. Just like in the kitchen the other day, a faint, papery shush too low to be more than a suggestion of sound.

The noise shivered over her, setting the fine hairs on her arms and the back of her neck on end. It was almost a vibration, and it was so intense she nearly wriggled, as if to get away from it. But instead she froze again, because the whisper was closer now.

Never leave you . . .

Never . . .

She shuddered at the plaintive voice. It was a woman, a woman caught somewhere between pain and pleasure, and when she squeezed her eyes shut she could see her.

A bare shoulder, glossy hair spilling over it as she moved . . . and then she was gone, and in her place was a pair of boots, falling into each other like drunken soldiers on the flowered carpet, their brown leather worn and scuffed, comfortably used.

Never leave you . . .

I promise . . .

Charlie gasped and curled her fingers in the comforter. A man's voice had answered, a foreign lilt audible even through the grit of passion.

She could still hear them, even if she could no longer understand them—there was only the faraway whisper of murmured words, the soft husk of breath over heated skin.

Behind her closed eyes, the images unspooled like an old filmstrip—a bare foot, arched and flexing, the soft rustle of sheer curtains at the window, hands clasped together on the rumpled red velvet bedclothes. And there was a soundtrack beyond the whispering, too. What sounded like horses' hooves on cobblestone, the distant cry of a gull, and a creaking groan that Charlie thought might be the wheels of a carriage.

Never leave me . . .

You must promise me . . .

Her breath caught in her throat. A single tear spilled down one cheek as she struggled up on her elbows, opening her eyes. As quickly as it had come, the heat dissipated with an audible rush, leaving her shivering.

And hearing that wrecked, broken voice in her head, murmuring, "Never leave me . . ."

* * *

Charlie didn't answer when Sam knocked, and for a moment he panicked. He had his bag over his shoulder and was standing on her porch assuming he would be welcome, and suddenly he wondered what the hell he was doing. What if she didn't want him here? What if she didn't want him here after he told her he was only staying for another two days?

What if, a voice in his head suggested, something had happened to her while he was out, and that was why she wasn't answering the door?

He was scrambling around the side of the house, finding it slow going in the drifts of snow, but he made it up the ice-thick back steps before he had a chance to think twice about it. The kitchen door was unlocked, which he would have to speak to her about later, and he dropped his bags inside just over the threshold, calling for her.

"Charlie? Are you here? Charlie?"

The house was quiet, the only noise the hum of the refrigerator and the rattle of the old windows in the winter wind. The afternoon sun glowed gold in the front parlor and on the honey-pine planks of the hallway floor.

It was too quiet, damn it.

"Charlie!" Sam shouted as he took the stairs two at a time. What if that angry thing had pushed her down? What if she had hit her head? What if she was unconscious?

What if . . . she was sitting at her desk, tapping furiously at her keyboard, the white snakes of iPod ear buds trailing over her shoulders.

"Charlie." He touched her shoulder, and she jumped a foot, one finger hitting the keyboard until a series of k's skidded across the screen.

"Sam!" She tugged the ear buds away and scrambled to her feet. Her face was flushed with what looked strangely like guilt. "You scared me to death."

"I knocked and I called, but you didn't answer," he said, cutting his glance sideways to read the computer screen.

Her chemise drifted to the floor in a cloud of white muslin as he watched, dark eyes hungry. Always so hungry, and for her.

She shivered under the weight of that gaze as it roamed over her bare skin. It was always so exciting to let him gaze at her before they touched, knowing that his hands, his mouth, would seek out every place his—

He glanced up sharply. "Mind if I read it? Too late. I did. Couldn't help it."

"What? No!" She stepped between him and the screen, blushing furiously now, and suddenly he understood the trace of guilt that tightened the lines of her mouth.

He grinned at her as he curled his fingers around her arms. "Are you writing a dirty book, Charlotte Prescott?"

She squeaked in response. Actually squeaked,

eyes wide behind her glasses, which were slightly askew, and cheeks flaming with color now. "No! God, Sam, of course not! I'm . . . I'm . . ."

He lifted a brow and smiled at her playfully. "Writing erotica?"

She smacked at his chest, but it was half-hearted. "It's not . . . that. It's . . . I don't know what it is."

He steered her out of the way and read over her shoulder. "His mouth would seek out every place his gaze had sought out, caressing her, mapping her body like an uncharted country, one he had conquered and would lay claim to time and again—"

"All right!" She pressed her lips together, caught somewhere between fury and embarrassment. "It's sexy, yes. But it's a love story. I think."

Reaching to one side, he grabbed for her rolling desk chair and sat down, pulling her onto his lap. For a moment, she refused to give, stiff and unyielding, but when he smoothed one hand up her back, she softened. "What do you mean, you think?" he asked, mouthing along her shoulder, making the cotton damp. "You don't know what you're writing?"

"Sort of." She let her head roll to one side, bumping gently against his, as he slid a hand under her shirt, fingers light on the supple skin over her rib cage. "It just started . . . coming to me. Oh."

He smiled against her collarbone as he smoothed the heel of his hand in lazy circles around one breast. The silk felt good against his skin. "Coming to you? What do you mean?" He punctuated the question with a biting kiss to her throat, pulling blood to the surface, knowing he would be able to see the pale purple bloom later.

"The characters just . . . came to me." Her voice was unsteady now that his free hand had slipped between her thighs. He used his thumb against the seam, searching out her clit. "Today . . ." She shuddered, pliant and nearly breathless now. "When I . . . went into the spare room."

This time she gasped instead of squeaked, which wasn't surprising since he shoved her out of his lap to stand up, mouth working in disbelief before he finally got the words out.

"You did what?"

"Butch came with me," she began, but he interrupted her.

"Oh right. The hero cat. I don't think he's going to protect you."

Charlie blew out a sigh that ruffled her hair a little. "He was trying to walk on the keyboard—"

Sam held up his hands. "Whoa. Next you'll be telling me Butch wrote this. He channels Barbara Cartland, right?"

"Shut up," she said exasperatedly. "Okay, if you won't listen, here goes." She looked into the monitor and poised her fingers above the keyboard, then started typing as if she was possessed.

* * *

"Do it," she whispered, letting her lips brush against Daniel's cheek. "No one can hear."

"You play with fire, my girl." He shook his head, his dark shaggy mane tickling her nose. "One day we'll both be burned."

"I don't care," she groaned, stubborn and aching, pressed against him in the dark shed, the silver moonlight thin and cold through the window. With a shaking hand she reached for the buttons of her bodice, slipped them loose one by one as he kissed the words out of her mouth, bit down on the plump swell of her bottom lip.

He wouldn't refuse her, she thought through the haze of need, trembling as it heated her. He could never refuse her.

Pulling apart her bodice, the chemise underneath it, she offered her breasts to him, pale and smooth in the dark. With one hand behind his head, fingers scrabbling in his hair, she tugged him down, and he went willingly, mouth fastening around one erect peak.

She groaned again, shameless, as his tongue pressed the rigid underside of her nipple against the roof of his mouth so he could draw hard, suckling. The sensation arrowed into her belly, a streak of fire, and she clutched his head harder as he sucked, pulling on her breast so deeply she felt her knees wobble.

"Daniel," she breathed, and hitched up her skirts with her free hand.

He didn't hesitate, didn't play at protest, simply slid his hand between her thighs, petting her

*once before his fingers parted her. When the first
one worked inside her, firm and hot, she shuddered. When his thumb found the swollen knot
of flesh above it, tracing around it in a lazy circle,
she cried out only to find his free hand clamped
over her mouth.*

*"Hush now, love," he whispered into the smooth
skin between her breasts. "Hush now and let me."*

*She nodded, a sob of helpless need stifled
behind his palm, and let him stroke her as she
shook and quivered there in the musty darkness,
the shed wall rough at her back, snagging at the
fabric of her dress.*

*She didn't care, she thought just before she
broke. She didn't care about anything but him,
and this.*

Sam looked at her with wonder. "That was
fast," he said.

"Like I said, it just comes to me. I don't know
how." Charlie gave him a worried look and then
turned away from her monitor screen.

Chapter Twelve

A stiff drink, Lillian decided as she walked home hours after lunch with Iris. Hours which had been spent in the headache-inducing heat of the historical society library as Iris led her through the Prescott family tree.

Gloria scuffed through the drifting snow on the cleared sidewalk, finding a dried leaf that was the same gingery russet as her coat. She snuffled and play-growled as she pranced, stopping every now and then to pounce.

"If you're seeing ghosts, too," Lillian muttered, "we're all doomed. Come on, you."

Gloria followed as she turned up the walk to Charlie's house. The good news was that Iris had been a veritable fount of information about Charlie's family; the bad news was that Lillian had been forced to endure her friend's gentle lectures and still had no idea what to make of the family tree and pages of anecdotes and historical details she had copied onto a miscellaneous assortment of scrap paper.

The best news, she thought as she rapped at the solid black door, would be if she could convince Charlie to open a bottle of wine.

Charlie didn't answer her knock, but when Lillian pulled away to glance at the window, she heard voices. Not ghostly voices, but very human ones—and both of them raised in the unmistakable volume of an argument.

"Oh, Charlie," she murmured under her breath. And knocked harder. Gloria helped out with a demanding yap.

The door flung open a moment later, and she blinked when found herself faced with a very tall, very angry Sam. He was answering Charlie's door now?

Before she could remark on just how ballsy she thought that was, Sam growled, "Lillian. Good. Maybe you can talk some sense into her."

"I heard that!" Charlie called from the other room, although honestly the decibel level of her voice was closer to shouting than calling. Lillian smiled tightly at Sam and pushed past him, Gloria following at her heels.

"What on earth is going on here?" she demanded when she found Charlie in the front parlor, pacing in front of the fireplace. "You two have only known each other for a few days, and if you're bickering like this already, I have to tell you, it's not exactly a promising sign."

"We're not bickering," Charlie protested, and Sam snorted. His blue eyes were blazing.

"Oh no? What do you call it?"

"I call it you being absurd and overprotective and . . . and stupid, and me being perfectly able to take care of myself, thank you very much," Charlie snapped.

"Stupid?" Sam retorted, crossing his arms over his chest. He was as flushed as Charlie was, and Lillian couldn't help watching as the muscles in his upper arms rippled with tension. "I'm being stupid when you're the one who decided to go hang out with the spooks while you were all alone in the house?"

Lillian glanced at Charlie, startled. She still wasn't convinced that the ghost or spirit or whatever the hell it was would truly hurt anyone, but that was the kind of thing no one should test on her own.

"Nothing happened," Charlie gritted out. She'd scooped her hair up on the back of her head in a loose knot and shoved a pencil through it as an anchor. It was her I-mean-business style, and Lillian hadn't seen it since the day Charlie had decided to clean out the house's enormous, dusty attic. "Nothing but the same heat I've felt before, except this time I heard them talking. I saw them."

"Them?" Lillian said, intrigued. She sat down on the sofa and spread her notes over the coffee table.

"A man and a woman." Sam didn't sound happy about this new wrinkle, either. "She saw, or she visualized, whatever you want to call it, a man and a woman, apparently in the throes of passion. It was all very inspiring, I understand."

Lillian glanced up at that, and bit back a smile when Charlie scowled. "I don't know what you're so upset about," she said, and turned around to press a hand against the window glass, needing the feel of something bracingly cold. "But you're making me crazy. And not in a good way."

Lillian turned a surprised laugh into a cough that she was pretty sure didn't fool either of them, and waved at him when Sam opened his mouth to protest. "Look, I'm not exactly sure what you two are fighting about, but I have some news. Any chance you two could call a cease-fire long enough for me to tell you about it?"

She glanced between the two of them when Charlie turned around again, and waited until they had both nodded before adding, "Good. Now. Is there any chance we could open some wine while I do?" She saw Charlie glance toward the spice rack in the kitchen and quickly said, "No, for God's sake, please don't mull it. I'm going to need all the help I can get."

"Where did you find all this?" Charlie asked Lillian a half hour later. They had all trooped in the kitchen, where Lillian had spread her notes over the wide expanse of the kitchen table and Sam had unearthed a bottle of pinot grigio Charlie was trying to pretend he hadn't turned up his nose at.

"I have friends in low places," Lillian told her with a waggle of her eyebrows. She took another long swallow of her wine and sighed in appreciation. "At the historical society, in fact. Iris Munson. I've known her forever, but the woman gives me a hell of a headache. Or maybe it's the heat in the place."

Charlie laughed ruefully. Lillian never failed to fascinate her, but she was still surprised that her new friend had taken such a fervent interest in whatever paranormal thing had taken up residence in the Prescott house. It would be one thing if Lillian had ever seemed like the type to find the supernatural believable, but the woman Charlie had gotten to know over the past two months was the last person she ever would have imagined could get hooked on ghost stories.

"What is all this?" Sam asked, sifting through the pieces of notepaper, each one covered with Lillian's spidery scrawl.

Charlie straightened her spine, metaphorically at least, and wondered if moving her chair away from his would be ridiculous. It would, of course it would, because this wasn't seventh grade, but she couldn't concentrate. Not with him so close, and smelling so good, and the memory of the heat of his body so fresh. She'd been this close to stripping off her clothes and letting him do her right there on her desk when he'd decided freaking out over her solitary trip to the spare room was more important than kissing her.

The big jerk.

"It's the Prescott family tree, among other things," Lillian said, pawing through the scraps herself, clearly looking for something. "I think it's probably pretty clear that this ghost, or ghosts, has to be a Prescott, right? Well, to begin with, you are from an interesting clan. I bet the most interesting genes got concentrated in you, Charlie."

Charlie didn't quite like the feeling of suddenly being under an electron microscope with naked DNA, even though she knew her neighbor didn't mean it that way. But she leaned forward to look at the pieces of paper Lillian had finally put in some kind of order.

"Here we go," Lillian announced. "Cyrus Prescott was married to Louisa Weston in the 1870s—it says the exact date right there on that photocopy of the church record but I can't read it without my glasses." Charlie peered at it without much interest. "Their children were Temperance, Constance, and one son, Merit. According to Constance's diary, which was found in the society's papers only recently, Temperance was, quote unquote, a fallen woman. Her lover's name was only indicated by the initial *D* wherever it appeared in the diary. But you probably know all that, don't you, Charlie? Do you know who the man was?"

Charlie's lips parted but she replied slowly, "No. I don't. How interesting." She'd heard of Constance, though the existence of a diary was news to her, and had heard of Merit, and had known vaguely that there was a third sibling. But never knew her name.

Temperance.

Feeling as shocked as if she'd been struck by lightning, she wasn't ready to reveal that in her automatic writing, her ancestress and her heroine were one and the same. Had Sam even seen the name? She didn't think so.

"Cyrus sounds like a laugh a minute," Sam said darkly from the other end of the table.

Charlie and Lillian ignored him as Lillian continued. "Merit married Abigail Avery, and their children were Patience, born in 1910, and your grandfather, James, born in 1912."

"I barely remember him," Charlie said softly, thinking of the fierce old man with the beaky nose and the faint scent of pipe tobacco clinging to his clothes.

"Patience married William Holbrook in 1935," Lillian went on, "but they never had children. William was building ships for the war effort by the time they were married a year or two, and he was later killed in a factory mishap."

Charlie made an involuntary noise, and tried not to flinch when Sam reached over and coasted a hand along her spine. More than one of the Prescotts had died too young, and for the first time she wondered why and if it had anything to do with whatever spirit lurked in this house. She shuddered involuntarily.

"Your grandfather James married Josephine Bale, and their children were Margaret, Michael, and May," Lillian concluded. "And you know most of the rest." She set down the notes and picked up her wine, brooding over the glass for a minute, her brows knitted in thought.

"I don't—" Sam began.

"The only ancestor who could be the ghost is Temperance. And if she had a lover, well, there's the second ghost," Charlie rushed out, not meeting Lillian's sharp gaze or explaining her reasoning. "So that's the family story no one would ever finish for me. Anything in the town records on what happened to her?"

The wind shook the window over the sink, the glass rattling with a brittle shiver. "No. Maybe that's what we need to figure out," Lillian said softly.

"I think we need to figure out more than that," Charlie said.

She stood up, arms wrapped around herself, for comfort as well as warmth. The sun was already going down, and she went to the side window. It was low over the water, glowing with gold fire.

"Like what?" Sam asked.

Charlie was lost in thought, feeling suddenly cold but from the inside out. If she and Sam were no more than channels for those long-ago lovers . . . then what had happened between them wasn't real and meant essentially nothing.

And if the ghosts were trying to send her a message, she didn't want to hear it.

"This may sound strange, but right now I wish that the past and the present were completely separate. And that they stay that way."

"Oh, honey, life isn't like that," Lillian said in a soft rush of worried words.

She turned around to face the others. Sam's face was set hard, the first shadow of stubble lining his jaw, his hair tousled where he'd run his hands through it restlessly. Lillian was staring into her wineglass, her eyes cast down.

"The past and the present—oh, they always connect somehow. But—" She looked up and around anxiously at the two of them. "We all seem to agree that supernatural beings have appeared, right?"

"Yes," Sam said bluntly.

Charlie nodded, hating, absolutely hating that her dreams of love actually belonged to someone else. Spectral entities who needed bodies seemed to be the easiest explanation. Or were they omens of love gone wrong that she was supposed to heed? She'd read most of Dickens, knew *A Christmas Carol* just about by heart, even if she hadn't been able to remember the name of the scariest ghost in it because Sam had been next to her at the time.

"Okay. My theory is that these spirits seem to care a lot about you," Lillian said. "Or maybe a better way of putting it is that they need you. Family ties are the strongest," she chirped. "Especially around the holidays."

"So I've heard," Charlie said dryly. "But none of the ghosts have identified themselves as Prescotts per se."

"Have you ever seen their faces?" Lillian asked.

"Ah—no." Charlie didn't want to describe

what she had seen and felt. Lillian seemed to know the gist of it.

"I was wondering if there were old tintypes of them in the town archives," Lillian mused. "I suppose I could ask Iris."

"Sure. Why not?" Charlie strove to keep her tone friendly, but the other woman's interest unnerved her for some reason. By this point, Charlie wanted only to believe that the ghost or ghosts were nothing more than reflections of her tendency to daydream.

That . . . and a stealthy loneliness that had crept up on her because it was December and Christmas was coming. It wasn't her favorite holiday and it never had been, but she'd always gotten through it somehow. Friends helped. So did keeping it simple.

And then along came Sam Landry, thanks to Franny. He was smart. Protective. Strong. Sexy. A keeper, most definitely. But he didn't seem to want to be kept. Of course, getting himself bashed by her resident ghosts wasn't a plus.

"Then I'm going to look for images," Lillian said decisively. "I am very curious about Temperance. She sounds very independent. A rare quality for her time."

Charlie shrugged. "Maybe it came down to me. I like being by myself."

She swallowed hard, tears prickling behind her eyes even as Sam stood up, striding across the room toward her. "But I guess ghosts get a little lonely too," she added. "So maybe my arrival woke them all up in time for Christmas."

Lillian looked completely dismayed. "I'm so sorry, Charlie. But we don't know what brought them back or what will happen." She hesitated. "Are you sure you want to stay here?"

She gave Sam a pleading look that Charlie didn't see.

"I mean it, I want you to pack a bag right now," Sam said, and slammed his hand down on the counter.

Lillian was gone, and Gloria with her. An hour of unfounded speculation on every leaf and twig of the Prescott family tree had taken them back to where they'd begun—with no more information than what Lillian had scribbled down that afternoon—and they were all tired and edgy. Charlie looked absolutely wrecked, and the only thing Sam wanted was to get her out of this house and into a nice warm bed somewhere.

Which was turning out to be a lot more difficult than he'd imagined, even if she had more or less acknowledged that their paranormal visitors had something to do with her family.

"Will you please knock off the caveman routine?" Charlie said now, edging away from him and pouring herself another glass of wine. "You can be Tarzan if you want to, but don't expect me to be Jane."

"I am not being a caveman," Sam snapped, and

took Charlie's arm. "I don't want you to get hurt. And when this argument started, you expressed some concern for me on that score. Remember?"

Charlie wriggled, trying to disentangle herself, but Sam held tight. She wasn't walking away from this conversation, not now.

"Nothing's ever happened to me," she said finally, and set down her wineglass to place her hands on his chest. They looked too small to him, even though he knew how strong they were when she was clutching at him, holding on as he pumped inside her. "You know that. I was lying in that room today and nothing attacked me. Nothing hurt me. I got a paranormal peep show, that's all."

"Yeah, well, you never knew there was a pushy ghost who liked to knock your boyfriends over, either," Sam argued.

"Singular." She gave him a thin smile. "Boyfriend. There's only you. And I'm not sure you qualify. You have to stick around for that."

"I'm trying to." His head was starting to pound, part wine and part aggravation. "This is a whole lot more than I bargained for."

"Maybe you shouldn't have knocked on my door," she said airily.

"Well, I did. And here we are."

She gave him a fierce look. "Sum it up for me, Sam. Where are we exactly?"

"At the beginning of"—he hesitated—"in the throes of—hell, I don't know what to call it. And I suspect you don't, either."

"I'm not even sure my mind is my own at this

point. All that red velvet and writhing around and mysterious stories that write themselves—"

"I saw your fingers move on that keyboard."

"You're my witness, hard-headed though you are." She blew out a sigh. "Next you'll become a devotee of rapping and I don't mean the music. Séance, anyone?"

He looked a little uncomfortable. "Well, that you started writing hot-n-sexy romance for no reason at all is a little unusual, don't you think?"

She only shrugged. "There's a market for it. Maybe I can sell it to a New York publisher. Saying that ghosts inspired me might interest one or two."

"I don't think so. They've heard it all. If there's anyone more cynical than an editor, I can't think who. Charlie, why won't you listen?"

He wasn't just exasperated, he was afraid, plain and simple. The idea of Charlie all alone here, recklessly encouraging the damn thing by hanging out in that room while he was away . . .

"Sam, come on." Charlie took advantage of his distraction to push away from him. "I'm not going to leave my own house. I have to deal with this. And it's . . . well, it's sweet that you're so concerned about me, but, well . . ."

She trailed off, face pinched closed, not even looking at him.

"I won't be around forever," he finished for her, and closed the distance between them again. "You're right."

His voice was harder than he'd meant it to be, harsher, too, the words sounding raw. She flinched when he grabbed her up again, craning his head down to look her in the eyes, forcing her to face him.

"In fact, I have to be out of here in two days," he said, and watched as surprise and disappointment and something much more brutal flickered through her eyes. "I have to write this goddamn article if I want to keep my job and if you haven't noticed, everyone's on the verge of being canned. I don't have a choice on that, but I want you to come with me. I want you with me, Charlie."

Too many unspoken things hung between them, and the air was charged with it, snapping fire in the silence.

But Charlie didn't back down, didn't soften beneath his hands, and he couldn't say he was really surprised. Charlie was made of much sterner stuff than she appeared to be, and it was one of the things he was beginning to love about her.

He flinched away from the thought at the same time she wrestled away from him again, and he didn't have time to examine it when she stalked to the other side of the room.

"And then what, Sam?" she said. She was trembling and pale, and he gritted his teeth, tightened his hands at his sides instead of going to her.

"We fell into bed like . . . well, I don't know what," she said, a little wildly. Her hair had come loose sometime in the last hour, and it fell around her face as she spoke. "I've never done anything like this before, I've never felt anything like this before. But you don't even live here. I don't even know what this is between us, or where it's going."

And that's when it struck Sam.

He'd felt that heat, too, the first night, and he wouldn't chalk it up entirely to ghosts. No way. That was them.

He'd wanted to kiss her, touch her, had breathed in all that sexual heat until he was on fire with it.

And now he couldn't keep his hands off her. Couldn't stop thinking about her. Was feeling like every other foolish, lovesick, overprotective man in history, when he hadn't had more than a meaningless weekend fling with a woman in years, because that was how he liked it.

Charlie had sagged into the chair Lillian had abandoned, and cradled her head in her hands. She looked exhausted, confused, and Sam didn't blame her. This thing between them had hit out of the blue, and it had happened right here in this house, where Charlie had come looking for peace and quiet, and had instead gotten ghosts and a horny reporter who kept pawing at her, not that she was complaining as far as he could tell.

This house, he thought absently. Where Charlie had gotten mysterious flashes of two passionate lovers, creating enough heat between them to melt a winter's worth of New England snow and ice.

She probably assumed that he thought she was crazy. Not even remotely. But he knew she'd bite his head off if he said so.

Without warning, his skin crawled. What if this wasn't even about them? What if this wasn't just an unexpected infatuation for him, and an uncharacteristic fling for her?

What if it was the ghosts, using them, energized by them, throwing them together?

He didn't know if that was possible, if it made any kind of sense, but he did know he needed to find out, for Charlie's sake as well as his own. Before one of them got hurt in ways that couldn't be patched up with an ice pack or a band-aid.

He kneeled next to her, smoothing a hand down her back until she looked at him. And there it was, need and desire and possessiveness rising up inside him like smoke, choking out every shred of common sense.

Almost.

"Charlie, you need to listen to me," he said. "I mean it. This may be more complicated than we realized, and I think we need to get out of the house, just for a day or—"

He pretended he didn't feel it coming, pretended that something hit him in the gut, so hard he toppled backwards, skidding across the floor.

He pretended a little too well. The world went black.

Chapter Thirteen

"Thanks for coming so quickly. He, um, was balancing on a chair," Charlie said weakly.

The EMT guy—his badge said Ricky Kascinski—looked to be about twelve, but he could certainly aim a skeptical look with the best of them. The other guy had gone out to the EMT vehicle to call in a report and put back some of the gear they'd brought in.

She realized the chairs were all upright and exactly where you'd expect them to be around the kitchen table.

Kneeling next to Sam, who was conscious after several heart-stopping moments of being slumped on the floor, Ricky mopped up the blood on Sam's head with an antiseptic wipe and slid a large gauze pad underneath it at the same time.

"He doesn't need stitches," Ricky said, and Sam grunted. "But he should see a doctor tomorrow. Tonight if he can't stay awake or you see any

other symptoms of concussion—" He reeled
them off for Charlie's benefit. "Just call us."

"Am fine," Sam muttered somewhat uncon-
vincingly, and groaned when he tried to sit up
further. He'd gone white as paper, and Charlie bit
her lip as she took one of his hands.

"You're going to need to watch him for several
hours off and on, for dizziness or confusion,
vomiting. And you can ice the lump on his head
in ten-minute intervals, to keep the swelling
down." Ricky peeled off his gloves and tucked
them into his kit with the sodden gauze, and then
stood up. His thick brown hair flopped over his
forehead as he leaned down to catch Sam under
one arm.

Charlie got up and did the same, staggering a
little bit as the two of them wrenched Sam to his
feet. He muttered through it, attempting to bat
Charlie's hands away, but he didn't protest when
she held on tighter.

"Is there somewhere comfortable to put him
until he recovers a little bit?" Ricky asked. "Got
a clean dishtowel for under his head?"

"Yes," she said, grabbing a folded one from a
shelf on their way out of the kitchen. "He can lie
on the sofa." Charlie helped Ricky steer Sam
through the hall and into the front parlor. He
sagged onto the sofa, still grumbling, but he let
himself be arranged on his back with a cushion
under his head.

Charlie walked Ricky to the door. "Thank you
so much," she said. Her heart was finally beating

normally again, or close to it, but she was still jittery. "Okay. Call us or call the hospital if there are changes in his condition."

She nodded. He'd gone over the list twice, after all. Once before Sam came to, and once after.

When Ricky was gone, she closed the door behind him and leaned against it for a fraction of a second, listening to the faint squawking of the radio as the EMT vehicle pulled away.

"Charlie?" Sam sounded like the tail end of a long day—rough and weak and fading.

She ran back into the parlor and sank to her knees beside the couch, laying an arm over his chest carefully. "What's the matter?"

"Nothing an ice pack won't fix," he said gruffly, and winced as he moved his head. He grabbed her hand when she started to move away, holding her in place. "So . . . like I was saying before we were so rudely interrupted . . ."

"I'll get my stuff," she said soberly, and kissed him before she ran up the stairs.

The tentative knock on Lillian's front door didn't get through the shriekingly dramatic opera flowing into her earbuds anymore than the EMT vehicle's siren had. It was Gloria who roused Lillian from an involving mystery novel, jumping on her chest with chunky little paws and pushing the book aside with her snout this time. The dachshund ran into the front hall, barking frantically. It was almost eight o'clock, and Lillian couldn't imagine who might have stopped by. She opened the door to find Sam leaning heavily on Charlie.

"What on earth . . . ?" Lillian said, and moved aside to let them in.

"Had a little run-in with our not so friendly apparition after you left," Sam said wryly, and let Lillian usher him toward the big easy chair near the fireplace.

"He hit his head," Charlie said, and to Lillian's surprise she burst into tears. "He was . . . unconscious. I called 911 and the EMTs got here right away—didn't you hear?"

"No," Lillian said, looking astonished and guilty. "I didn't even see the flashing lights. When I get into a book—oh, never mind."

"Anyway, we didn't want to stay for a second longer than it took to pack a few things and get out," Charlie said, a little breathlessly.

Sam was too tactful and too whacked to mention the argument that had led to his taking such drastic action. But Lillian was staring at him, her eyes fixed on the area above his belt. "Your shirt is heaving," she said.

"That would be Butch," he explained. "Charlie realized the cat carrier was in the spare room."

He unbuttoned a couple of the topmost buttons and the older woman took a peek inside.

"That cat sure looks comfortable."

"I'm not. He likes it so much he's digging his claws into my abs," Sam complained.

"You'll both live," Lillian said with maternal

firmness. She'd turned her gaze on Charlie, who looked like she was about to faint.

Lillian tugged her into her arms and let the girl spill her fear and relief onto her shoulder, wet, hot tears soaking into her sweater. Sam was trying to stand up, and Lillian waved him down with one hand, scowling. "Stay where you are."

"Oh, Lillian . . ." Charlie sobbed out a few more incoherent words.

"It's all right, sweetheart," she hushed Charlie, rubbing soothing circles against her friend's spine. The girl was too thin, and she felt terribly break-able in Lillian's arms. "It's okay. I'd bet money it would take a lot more than that to do Sam any serious injury."

"Hey," Sam said mildly, but he smiled, too. Butch poked his pointy-eared head out to get a little fresh air, then settled back down, slithering around inside the shirt.

Sam looked like hell. Smeared blood stained his collar and the back of his shirt, and he was too pale, his hair still slightly sweaty and tousled, circles under his eyes that hadn't been there a few hours ago.

And Charlie didn't look much better when she finally untangled herself from Lillian's embrace. Her glasses were smudged with fingerprints and tears, and Lillian removed them gently before steering Charlie onto the sofa beside Sam's chair.

"Sit down for a minute and let me make some tea, sweetheart." She turned around and saw the bags on the floor in the entry hall, and smiled.

The pair of them were like a couple of bedraggled orphans coming in from the storm, and she was so pleased they had come to her, even though she lived right next door, she had to bite back a foolish grin.

But on her way into the kitchen, she offered up a silent remark to the one person she hoped might care. *I'm here for Charlie, Michael. And I'm so happy to be her friend.*

"Are you comfortable?"

"Stop fussing, girl," Sam growled, and pulled Charlie closer. Lillian's guest room boasted a big old bed with a pitted brass frame and hand-stitched quilts, and comfortable wasn't the word. Blissful was closer.

Of course, he knew that wasn't really what Charlie meant, but he was determined to distract her from his minor injury. As far as convincing her to leave the house went, his unexpected sprawl into the cabinets had certainly done the trick, although he would have preferred not to actually pass out. Jesus. He must have connected with a hell of a lot of force.

His head still ached, a deep, vibrating throb that hadn't really let up even with ice and ibuprofen. And the truth was that his point about the ghost hurting someone had certainly been proven. But he didn't want Charlie terrified, which was the distinct impression he got when he opened his eyes to find a strange guy examining his head and

Charlie crouched on the floor beside him, looking very serious.

He wanted her to be. He needed her to take this thing seriously, especially when one of the god-damned spooks seemed determined to shove him around the house at every opportunity. But he didn't want her so terrified she was frazzled, because if anything that would make her sloppy, too distracted to pay attention.

And he wasn't going to be around forever. That was just the plain truth.

He tightened his arm around her as she snuggled closer, laying her head on his chest. She was warm and pliant beside him, all the lines of her body finally loose and relaxed as she let him stroke down her back and nuzzle into her hair.

"You need to sleep," she murmured, already sleepy, the words fanned warm against his chest as she breathed. "But you should wake me up if you wake up, and I'll get you more ice and pills, okay?"

"I'll be fine, baby." He kissed the top of her head, breathing in the sweet apple smell of her shampoo. "You need to sleep, too, and stop worrying."

She pressed lazy, soft kisses to his chest, her eyelashes fluttering against his skin like delicate wings. "It's a little tough when something keeps knocking you out when you come over, you know?"

"Hey!" He reached down to pinch her ass

lightly. "I've only been knocked out once. Total lucky shot."

"Don't joke about it, Sam," she said, and got up on one elbow. In the silver moonlight, her eyes were huge and sad. "This is serious."

He didn't answer, just tugged her toward him and lowered his mouth to hers. She opened for him willingly, letting him lick lazily into her mouth, curl his tongue around hers, ease her into submission against him. Draping a leg over both of his when he urged her up, she kissed him back, until there was nothing but their mouths, connected wet and hot and endless.

But . . . comfortable, too. Not urgent, he realized. This was comfort, this was reassurance, not the hungry need he'd felt every other time they'd kissed like this.

And it made him wonder. What if that demanding, overwhelming need really was something the spirits had fed into them? What if the incredible sex had been nothing more than two ghosts acting out a long-ago passion and using their bodies?

He let his mouth fall away from Charlie's, and she subsided back onto his chest with a contented sigh. The sound was so intimate, so happy, he could feel it warm in his bones, his veins.

And that was odd, too. Because if he didn't need to have her right this minute, hot and hard and right now, what did it mean that this easy familiarity, this contentedness felt so right?

He frowned as she snuggled deeper, getting

comfortable, her breathing already slowing and deepening as she eased toward sleep.

He didn't want this. He didn't need this. He didn't even believe in this. But he was pretty sure, lying in Lillian's guest room with a woman he hardly knew, that he was falling in love.

"Okay, here's my itinerary," he said softly. "You wanted to know it, right?"

"Aren't you romantic," she whispered. "And the answer to your question is no, not now. Besides, you're in no shape to travel."

"Granted." He pulled her closer. "And I will wait until I can drag a comb through my hair without bleeding from the scalp."

She snorted into his chest. "I'm beginning to think you're not as smart as I thought."

"I can live with that," he replied. "Anyway, I have to go to Narragansett, there's a weeping woman ghost there, then to Gloucester for an ectoplasmic manifestation that could be a man or a giant jellyfish, I can't remember. Then back here."

"Can't any of that wait?"

"No. Kevin, my boss, has hinted that I will be fired if I don't get these interviews and get this story. I swear he has a GPS chip planted in my cell to track me."

She patted his chest. "Let me talk to him."

"I don't think that would be a good idea," Sam said hastily.

"Mind if I ask why?"

"Because he's a punk. And he has an assistant

who is apparently named Angel Pants. You wouldn't like them."

"You may be right," she agreed with a soft sigh. "Well, do you still want me to come with you?"

He dropped a kiss on her tousled hair. "I don't want you to stay in your house until I get back. Think you can handle that?"

She nodded, brushing his nipple absentmindedly with her lips.

"I'll travel faster if I'm alone," he explained. "I'm used to working that way. Nothing personal."

"Of course not," she murmured. She was just glad he really was all right. But she did intend to use her womanly arts to keep him on the island for another day. "Now don't move. And no reciprocating." Charlie slid down his body and began.

After several minutes of what she was doing, Sam groaned in ecstasy. She slid back up and nestled contentedly under his arm, and they fell asleep together.

By tomorrow evening, he looked pretty much as he had on the day she'd met him. Gorgeous. A little raffish. And good to go.

"Bridget Hartigan is about eighty, from the sound of her," he reassured Charlie.

"Okay. It's your job, you have to do it, I'm not going to whine."

"Thanks." He planted a tender kiss on her lips.

"But I want to whine," she said when he'd stopped. "Just so you know. I will miss you. Hurry back."

"I will." He patted the breast pocket of his

parka. "Got the ferry schedule right here, you're on speed dial, and Lillian is going to keep an eye on you." He grinned before he shouted to her in the next room. "Right, Lillian?"

"Right," came the abstracted answer.

"She's going through the new releases catalog," Charlie said. "Summer book orders are coming up already."

"Really?" Sam said. "And I haven't done my Christmas shopping. What do you want?"

So they were going to get that far, she thought suddenly. "Just you," was all she said.

"Okay," he answered evenly. "I'm looking forward to it."

She glanced at the clock on the mantel. "You have about half an hour before you have to go."

"Got that ferry schedule memorized, I see."

Charlie laughed. "It's not that complicated. On the hour this time of year, going and coming."

He set down his laptop case and eased his parka off. "I'm going to lose ten pounds if I stand here sweating. So ask the big question, whatever it is."

Sam grinned at her but she didn't grin back. "You're just happy because you know there's a time limit here."

"Yeah. That's right. Sorry, it's a guy thing. So what did you want to ask me that won't keep for a day and a half?"

Charlie patted his chest. His shirt was a bit damp and he hadn't been kidding about the sweating. "Just about your family. You sort of said you weren't going to see them at Christmas, but I was wondering if they were in Boston or around there. You did mention going up there once to investigate us Prescotts, and—"

"I grew up outside the city. Upscale suburb. Big stone houses, perfect lawns. I used to call it Deadwich, because it might as well be," was his unemotional reply. "And I won't be stopping in. My dad made it clear a while ago that I was a grave disappointment, blah blah blah, and my mom goes along with whatever he says. No brothers or sisters."

"Oh. Well, we don't have to talk about it. Sorry if I touched on a sore spot."

He reached out to her, taking her by the hand. "Not really. I deal with it in my own way, just keep moving on."

Did he mean that being a roving reporter suited him or that he literally just kept moving? It didn't seem like the time to ask squirrelly female questions, so she dropped the subject, settling for non-verbal reassurances that he seemed a lot more comfortable with.

Hugs. Kisses. And a look in his eyes that was simultaneously masculine and vulnerable. It melted her.

Chapter Fourteen

His departure meant she was alone most of the day, because Lillian was at the bookstore. Charlie could have gone in and helped but she didn't want to. They were together from evening to morning coffee as it was, and she didn't want to wear out her welcome.

Butch the cat had made peace with Gloria the dachshund with astonishing speed, and they slept together in the overstuffed armchair.

But her own house called to her. She looked at it every time she went by a window. It didn't seem scary or forbidding, just oddly empty.

As if it were waiting for everyone to return. She had to wonder if the ghosts were banging around inside it. She'd left lights on against her eventual return, and she was pretty sure they didn't like lights.

Charlie had scarcely wanted to think about Temperance Prescott or her lover, Daniel. Who-ever he was.

Lillian and Iris would undoubtedly ferret out more information but she wasn't sure she wanted to know it.

Just thinking about them evoked fragments of her red-velvet vision and the half-glimpsed bodies in it passionately intertwined. She had a feeling that writing about it would not enable her to let go of the memory. No, it would only encourage the spirits to return.

They hungered for the life they'd had and the love they'd known. She had no doubt of that. There were tantalizing threads of recollection in what she'd seen that told her, when she thought about them without Sam there to get her all stirred up, that the crucial part of Temperance and Daniel's story had happened around Christmas.

She didn't know how she knew it, just that she did.

Charlie gave a start when she heard the phone ring inside the house, and ran to answer it.

"Hello—I mean, Lillian Bing residence," she said, quickly correcting herself.

"Yikes," Lillian said cheerily. "That sounds like a college dorm."

Charlie laughed. "Well, it sort of is at the moment. What's up?"

"Slow day at the store," Lillian said. "I'm turning it over to Jamie and you're coming with me to the historical society."

"I am?"

"Excuse me a sec—may I help you? Oh, Jamie,

could you take care of this customer? Thanks
so much."

She heard Lillian talking and waited for her to
get back to the phone.

"Charlie? Sorry. Yes, we can go today."

Lillian said it as if it was something Charlie
very much wanted to do, she noticed.

"Iris gave me the key so we'll have the place to
ourselves, bless her heart. But we can only stay
an hour. There's a sales rep coming in to the store
later and I want to see him."

Charlie took a deep breath. She wanted to say
no, but if Iris Munson had gone to the trouble
and Lillian was free, she didn't really have a
choice.

"I'll meet you there," Lillian added, quickly
giving Charlie the location and hanging up before
she could wiggle out of it.

Charlie sighed and hung up on her end. It would
be interesting to find out more, much more, about
her wayward ancestor, if they could. There was the
diary that Temperance's sister Constance had
kept. That promised to be the most interesting
of all.

It was the chance of stirring up the ghosts again
that bothered her. She didn't want to be pursued
by them down the quiet streets—especially since
whoever saw her would not see them. It seemed
that only she and Sam had perceived them so far,
and Charlie wanted to keep it that way.

* * *

Booted, mittened, protected by a pom-pomed knit hat that went down to her eyebrows, Charlie made her way down a side street of Edgartown to the saltbox house that housed the historical society. It was adorned with a ship's wheel and a tastefully lettered sign. She knocked on the door, stamping her feet on the mat, and heard Lillian call out to her from inside.

"Coming!"

She flung open the door and Charlie stepped inside on a gust of cold air that reminded her for just a second of the manifestations in the spare room. She shook the thought away as she divested herself of her coat and the rest of it. That had happened inside and wasn't normal. A butt-freezing blast off the Atlantic, even on a side street, was to be expected.

"The curator left the archive boxes that Iris and I were going through on a table for us," Lillian was saying.

"Okay. That was nice of him. Or her."

"Him. Mr. Bridge is awfully nice."

Charlie followed her to the table that held five lidded boxes made of beige cardboard with metal trim, lined up in a neat row. It was by a sunny window that was nonetheless drafty.

"Too cold?" Lillian asked, seeing Charlie shiver as they reached the table. "We could move, but the light is so good here and some of the documents are almost indecipherable. Mr. Bridge was wondering if the ink in the diary was homemade. It's faded badly."

"Maybe we shouldn't read it in the sunlight."

An out? Not a chance that Lillian would let her take it, Charlie thought.

"The overheads are rather dim once you move back into the room," Lillian said worriedly. "I think it will be all right and it's just for this once. Do you know, this will be only the second time that diary's been opened."

"Really?"

Lillian nodded. "Iris undid the ribbon and it was easy to see from the bright color inside the knotted part that no one ever had. Mr. Bridge was of the opinion that the diary hadn't been opened in over a hundred years. It was dated when it was donated."

"And when was that?"

"Oh, fifty years after Constance's death. I'd have to look at the cataloging document in it to give you the exact year."

"So anyone mentioned in it would have been long dead by then, too," Charlie pointed out.

"Yes, most likely. And it may have been simply swept up with a lot of other papers and stored in an attic somewhere, then surfaced in the town archives."

Charlie still felt a little uneasy. It had occurred to her that something about her had triggered the appearance of the ghosts in the first place. And if she were to handle something that at least one of them might have touched in their lives, the action could bring them here, out of the Prescott house.

The serene setting of the society's archive

room didn't seem like the place for passionate spirits. If Temperance and Daniel showed up, they might be better behaved. Or not.

She hoped the strong sunlight would keep the shadows at bay. "Did you—feel anything when you opened it?" she asked Lillian.

"No," the older woman said, "but then I'm not a Prescott." She smiled as she pulled a chair out for Charlie and then one for herself.

Charlie sat and let Lillian take the lid off a box, glancing at the yellowing, deckle-edged papers that the older woman took out with both hands, carefully setting them aside and covering them with the lid of the box to protect them from the sun. "Those are birth and death records," she said. "Marriages, property transfers, things like that, too. They were prosperous, generally speaking. Pillars of the community."

"I thought only the Prescotts owned the house I inherited."

"Yes, that's true. Iris checked on that."

Nice old ladies made the best snoops, Charlie thought with an inward smile. She'd bet good money that Iris and Lillian were experts at it.

"The Prescotts owned land that other people farmed outside of Edgartown and they held the title to other small houses in town."

"So the diary didn't necessarily come from my house," Charlie said thoughtfully. "I'm assuming they let their grown children live in one of the others."

"That's probably true," Lillian said. "I can't

confirm it, though, without reading each and every one of these documents."

"Don't bother if we only have an hour."

"I wasn't going to," Lillian replied. "I just wanted to get to the bottom. I'm looking for tintypes if there were any. Wouldn't it be fun if we could see what Temperance looked like?"

Charlie surveyed the five boxes. Plain as they were on the outside, they held a wealth of secrets.

"I think so."

Lillian shot her an appraising look. "Do you think you would recognize her from what you saw or sensed?"

"I really don't know," Charlie answered truthfully. The thought was a little alarming. She was becoming more and more convinced that the past ought to stay where it was—in the past.

But she knew her curiosity would get the better of her when it came to the diary that Constance Prescott had kept. When Lillian finally lifted out the small, clothbound book and put it in her hands, Charlie sat for a moment just holding it.

An unmistakable energy flowed from it, but she didn't want to tell Lillian that. The sensation she got was of swirling emotion, entirely female, as if a lifetime of feelings had been poured into the diary, then closed away. Whoever had donated it might not have been a Prescott or even married to a Prescott. Just someone clearing out their attic who'd seen a box of old papers and thought to donate it to the historical society.

"It wasn't with all this material to begin with,"

Lillian was saying. "They had found it in another box when they were cataloging its contents. Quite recently, too. Mr. Bridge happened to remember that it had been set aside so it could be returned to the Prescott papers. He brought it over to Iris right away."

"Do they find many diaries?"

Lillian gave her a thoughtful look. "Do you know, I asked him the same thing. He said they didn't. Or that the few they did get tended to be terse records of daily life. Valuable to historians, of course." She winked. "But to people like us, who love a good story, not as interesting. Constance's diary was her confidante, I think."

Did she dare open it and read? It seemed in an odd way like a violation of someone's privacy. Charlie touched the cover with her fingertips, noting the worn edges and the cracked spine. But it had been well-made, bound in limp leather with sewn-in pages. She didn't see any missing ones or torn-out parts when she riffled through it without reading and then closed it again, looking at the edges.

Whatever story it told was complete in its way. Still she hesitated, not wanting to tell Lillian why. If she hadn't been a direct descendant of the author's family, she might feel differently, Charlie thought.

This little island cherished its past and made every effort to preserve it—but maybe, Charlie mused, sometimes doing that made it hard for the past to be over.

She gave an almost inaudible sigh and opened it to the first entry. The handwriting was girlish, but there was something narrow and mean about it. Charlie pored over the faded writing, thinking that the diarist revealed more about herself than she did about the people in her life. Reading more rapidly, Charlie picked up many mentions of Temperance. Constance, who was evidently plain by her own estimation, had been jealous of her sister, who was beautiful and had many suitors to her sister's one.

"Interesting, isn't it? Are you finding out more about Temperance?"

"Not very much, unfortunately. But it's clear that her sister didn't like her."

"How sad," Lillian murmured, absorbed in her own task.

Charlie continued to read while Lillian looked through the Prescott papers once more and then moving on to a different box. "I want to find those tintypes," she murmured, humming to herself while she searched through that box, closed it up and chose a third.

Charlie's eyes widened. Bingo. Halfway through, Constance had launched into exactly what they were looking for: an account of her sister's elopement with a young man who was identified only as D.

"Daniel," she whispered to herself.

"What?" Lillian asked absently.

"Nothing. Just talking to myself. How much of the diary did you read?"

"Only a little. I would love to transcribe it but it would take weeks. Maybe you could do it, dear. Here, of course. I don't think Mr. Bridge would let you take it home."

"I wouldn't want to."

She was absorbed in the story of the elopement. It was difficult to read the fine, fading script, but it went quickly once she got the hang of it.

Even though Constance's tone was spiteful, the details seemed accurate enough. The affair between Temperance and Daniel had begun in fall and continued into winter—a moderate winter, something like the one they were having now, but the year had ended with a howling three-day blizzard that left the town buried in snow. Apparently the lovers had run away on Christmas Eve, from what she could tell—Constance had not dated every entry and Charlie wasn't sure her count was right. Had they been lost in the storm?

Charlie flipped back and forth in the diary. Constance had a tendency to ramble and digress, but then she wasn't writing a book. This and that caught her eye—many of the descriptions of Edgartown still fit, for one. But those were brief. It was marriage that preoccupied Constance Prescott, who was nervous about her chances and had filled the previous pages with details of the modest weddings of friends. But Temperance, her sister noted, was too impetuous and passionate to make a match to a suitable man.

With so little time to read it, Charlie tried to memorize a few lines to share with Sam. *My sister's clothes are too showy, Mother says. Temperance is the talk of the town. She wears red too often.* That would be a cause for scandal in a small, isolated community. *Temperance has angered Father most extremely—he vows to lock her in her room if she contradicts him again.* That was the first entry that gave a clue as to why Temperance might be haunting the Prescott house. Charlie straightened up and read more that seemed to have been in haste. The page was marred with drops and splotches of ink and the pen nib had left scratches. *His name is D—! I dare not write it out. And she has vowed to meet him in some secret place—I have found her diary, though I put it back in its place of concealment.*

Why hadn't she dared to write the young man's name? It seemed that nothing else had been sacred. Had Constance tattled? The Prescott sisters had been young women at the time, but her dislike and distrust of Temperance seemed close to an obsession.

Charlie didn't know what had ultimately happened, but she was dying to find out. The time frame of that part of the diary was the same as theirs in the present day—the weeks leading up to Christmas. Like the weddings, that too had been celebrated in a much more modest way back then. But some of the traditions were familiar.

Interspersed with the other December entries were pages devoted to the making of sweets like pulled taffy and peppermints. And pudding, including a list of ingredients. Flour. Eggs. Raisins and other preserved fruits. Suet. Charlie made a face. Sugar. Cheesecloth to roll the doughy lump in so it could be hung to steam over boiling water for hours. She didn't envy the Prescott cook.

Looking for more bits about Temperance, she kept reading as if caught in a spell, feeling somehow protected by the maternal presence of Lillian, who was carefully opening the lid of a flat, longish tin.

"Eureka!" she cried. "Charlie, look!"

"What?" Charlie closed the diary and set it aside and leaned over the tin, seeing the names written in a delicate hand under small oval tintypes.

There was the paterfamilias, Cyrus Prescott, a middle-aged man with a stern look and bristling muttonchops. His wife. Their children taken as a trio and separately. As young children and when they were grown. Constance. Merit. And Temperance.

The paper that framed them, printed with a calligraphic equivalent of a gilt frame, was fragile and crumbling, but the images themselves were remarkably clear, as sharp as digital photos. Charlie almost didn't want to look at Temperance.

Holding the tintype with great care, Lillian held that one up.

"Oh my," she said almost reverently. "Look at those eyes. She really was beautiful."

Charlie looked, relieved to see that there was no resemblance between them. But Lillian was right about her eyes. They held all the passion her sister wrote of so bitterly and intelligence as well.

For her portrait sitting, Temperance wore a buttoned-up, high-necked dress that fit like a second skin over what looked like an incredible figure, even perched stiffly on an ornate chair as she was. Leave it to the Victorians to show what was underneath without revealing an inch of skin, Charlie thought. Was this the woman she'd seen entangled in red velvet in her waking dream?

"Would you like a closer look?" Lillian extended the small tintype to Charlie so that she could take it if she wanted to.

She shook her head. "It's probably best if we don't handle this stuff too much," she said. But she was memorizing every detail of Temperance's lovely face—and, most of all, her manner. There was grace even in her conventional pose, and one silk-shod foot peeped out from under her voluminous skirts, as if she were on the verge of standing up and running away. Charlie told herself not to be so fanciful. But it was true enough that Temperance looked just as alive now as she had been when the tintype was taken.

"Oh, of course. I'll just put Tempy by you so you can see it better." Lillian put the tintype down on the table and held up the one of Cyrus. "Now he has a severe expression, doesn't he?"

"Yes." Charlie did think that Lillian seemed determined to have her look closely at the image of Temperance. Her gaze moved from the young beauty to her stern father, and she could see why Temperance would have to elope.

She wondered whether Daniel, whoever he

was, had gone to her father to ask for her hand and been refused. The diary was bound to mention if so. She thought to look at it again, but Lillian had picked it up from where Charlie had set it aside and was putting it back in the first box.

She set the lid on top and closed it with a thoughtful pat.

"I have to go," she said regretfully. "I'm not sure if you can stay, but Mr. Bridge probably wouldn't mind—"

"No," Charlie said quickly. She was glad the diary and the tintypes were back in their boxes. If Temperance and Daniel had appeared in her house and on her computer, she had the strangest feeling that the process might happen in reverse and she would be drawn into the pages of this diary, never to be seen again.

The ghosts in her house hadn't gone away, she was sure of it. They were just waiting for Sam to return. The parallel story that had begun so long ago still had no ending in her mind. Just processing all that she'd read and seen on this table was going to take her a while.

If only he were here to hug her . . . she thought of him with a warmth that suffused her and chased away the odd, chilly uncomfortableness of prying that reading the diary had given her. There was no doubt in her mind that Constance had been the sort of person who peered through keyholes and listened at doors.

"I mean, no thanks. I'll come with you. Mind if I stay at the store and walk home with you?"

"Not at all," Lillian said, rising. "I think the Prescott archive is more than history to you, Charlie. Am I right?"

"Yes," Charlie admitted reluctantly.

"I almost forgot to ask," Lillian continued. "Of course, we didn't have much time, but did you find anything that would explain why Temperance might be our restless ghost?"

Charlie nodded. "I think so, but I really have to come back and finish reading. I just might transcribe it—do you think Mr. Bridge would let me?"

"Of course," Lillian said warmly. "He'd be thrilled. Nobody uses the archives except old ladies and the occasional genealogical researcher. He'd be delighted to meet the last of the Prescotts—oh dear. I shouldn't put it that way, Charlie, it sounds so grim. I'm sorry."

"But I'm not the last, not by a long shot." Charlie walked with Lillian to where they'd left their coats and warm things. "Don't forget the cousins."

"Of course," Lillian said absently. "I just never did connect with them the way I've connected with you—I mean, they didn't talk to me when they did live here, except in passing. And they haven't come back to the Vineyard for years. I don't know if anyone's heard from them."

Probably not, unless the whole town read each other's mail, Charlie thought.

And, for a fleeting second, Charlie considered the thought that Lillian Bing had a history of her own. She'd ask her about it some other time, though. For now, they had to leave everything as they'd found it.

They put everything back where it had come from and left all five boxes on the table.

Sam Landry shut off his mini recorder after listening to the playback, rubbing his eyes. The ectoplasm thing had been a bust, just as he'd expected. The goofy guy who'd found it oozing from his cellar wall had even dared him to touch it.

Not feeling big and bold, Sam had poked a finger at it. Who the hell knew what it was? He just couldn't get excited. It felt like a blob, was all. He'd snapped a few photos that weren't going to make page one of *Scoop*. Blobs just didn't cut it. Blondes with big boobs always had, always would. Mafia guys, sometimes. But these days, they'd been elbowed aside by former CEOs and disgraced hedge fund kings doing the perp walk. If you could get one of those guys with a boobalicious blonde pleading for her man while she socked a cop with her Gucci bag, you'd hit pay dirt and a syndication sale.

He wondered who Kevin had assigned to all of the above, while he was relegated to this ridiculous gig, then realized that he actually didn't care.

Charlie Prescott was a lot more pleasant to think about. And to come home to, when he was done with the weeping ghost. He shook himself like a big cat, as if to rid himself of the whole damn circus of specters and hauntings and ectoplasmic whatevers.

He couldn't wait to drop off his rental car, which reeked of cigarette smoke anyway, and hop on the earliest ferry he could get back to the Vineyard.

What he wanted more than anything else was to lie next to her sweet warmth and silken skin. Whisper whatever it was she wanted to hear, listen to her soft voice responding with all the passion she hid under that demure manner of hers.

Wow. She had fire and it wasn't all that deep down. All he had to do was touch her just right and—bring it on. He could handle her, give her the utmost in pleasure, love her back . . .

Shut up, he told himself angrily.

Charlie hit the local history section at Pages, browsing through the titles one by one, looking for more information about Edgartown during the time of the diary. She had several books open on the shelves, going back and forth and comparing them with her mental notes, amused to find names that she'd seen in the diary, of shopkeepers and tradespeople, ministers and congregations, and those hauled into court by the constable. Apparently people were stealing lobster pots even then. Gossipy Constance must have read the newspapers of the day avidly. She seemed to love ferreting out sin and wickedness wherever she found it . But Charlie found no references at all to Temperance Prescott.

Had her father somehow managed to expunge her from the records of the town once she had eloped?

Charlie was also looking for information about the unknown Daniel. Around here it was a common enough name, but she suspected he hadn't been from Edgartown or anywhere near it.

She imagined him as a New York dandy, up to the Vineyard for a seaside vacation in the summer to clear a lingering catarrh—she loved the word, because it sounded exactly like what it was, a bad cold. *Catarrrrrrrrrrrh*. You could clear your throat just by saying it. She flipped through the books she'd set out as if she might find Daniel in the insert pages of old images, from early tintypes to the more newfangled photography on glass plates.

The beach photos showed fishermen and strollers, none of whom were named in the captions. And there were many images of the townsfolk, stacked up like firewood for group shots. The Ladies Auxiliary. The Edgartown Rowers. The ragtag but indomitable-looking soldiers who'd volunteered to defend the Union, and sadly, a lone image of the cemetery that some of them had returned to. There was no way she'd be able to pick out Temperance or Daniel in that sea of faces.

He'd probably seen her on the street somewhere and tipped his hat, starting a conversation with a small-town beauty who longed for a different life—*oh, stop writing their story,* she told herself silently.

If only they could tell it to her themselves.

Charlie closed up the books one by one, and put them back on the shelves. She was just too restless to stay at Pages any longer, and she slipped out while Lillian was talking to the sales rep in the back room, leaving her a note. She walked around Edgartown, thinking about Temperance and her sister doing the same thing. Carriages instead of cars, painted signs and no neon—it was easy to put herself in their shoes.

She distracted herself by looking in shop windows, grateful to hear instrumental arrangements of Christmas carols so they wouldn't get stuck in her head too soon in the season.

An antique store featured an old oil painting in the window of a young woman with a swan neck and piled-up hair. It wasn't Temperance, of course, though something about the pose made Charlie think of her. She felt a slight, rueful smile curve her lips. That tempestuous person was back inside the flat tin box safely hidden away at the historical society.

She thrust her mittened hands deeper in her pockets and walked on. She was going to have to go back, but she would bring Sam along the next time if that was all right with Mr. Bridge. She was sure Sam would be intrigued by the tintype of the beautiful Temperance, as notorious in her way as a misbehaving starlet, although only for wanting to marry the man she loved.

Daniel remained a mystery. But Charlie wasn't sure if Sam would be as interested in him.

Then an unexpected fragment of a melody floated through the air to Charlie, a few stanzas from a Christmas carol she loved and remembered the words to. She imagined Temperance hearing the same song when she ran away with her Daniel on Christmas Eve.

. . . the hopes and fears of all the years are met in thee tonight . . .

She sang it under her breath as she hurried back to Lillian's house.

Chapter Fifteen

Was she ever glad to see Sam. Charlie went straight into his arms when Lillian let him in. And how wonderful it was that he'd come over on an early morning ferry after dropping off his rental car in Falmouth. They would have the whole day alone together. Lillian was on her way to Pages and she already had her coat on.

"Hi, sonny," she said to Sam, pinching his cheek. She wrapped a handwoven scarf around her head until she became mostly a nose. "How do I look?"

"Toasty," Charlie said, not wanting to seem too eager for her friend to leave her own house.

"I am toasty." Lillian added thick-cuffed gloves to the ensemble and left with a wave to both of them.

"Welcome home. I missed you so much," Charlie murmured to Sam, nestling against him. His hands were cold, even though he'd worn gloves, which were now off. He was running them up and down her sweatered back to warm them up.

"Same here," he said, giving her fast little smooches on the cheek, chin, top of her head—his lips were cold, too.

"Let's go back to bed," she offered, sticking her hands down the back of his jeans and treating herself to a feel of two rock-solid butt cheeks. At least her hands weren't freezing and he certainly seemed to enjoy what she was doing. Sam tilted his hips closer to her, and she was equally pleased to feel his instant erection against her belly. Tall men were fun to play with, she thought mischievously, although all things were equal lying down.

Which was where they found themselves only minutes later.

"Let me," she begged, pushing his hands away from his shirt buttons.

"Wouldn't this be easier if I was standing up? You knocked me flat," he protested.

"Like I could. You wanted me to."

He'd stood there with his hands on his hips and the back of his knees against the edge of the brass bed. Booted feet apart, sturdy thighs tensed, and grinning wickedly, he'd told her to try.

And then he'd gone over like a falling tree, taking her with him. She'd landed on top, straddling his muscular middle. Didn't seem to bother him—she'd bounced a little with his laughs.

"Okay," he sighed happily, holding up his hands in surrender. "Undress me."

"First I get to strip."

She stood up over him on the bed, a little unsteady, but able to get off her clothes and fling them on the floor. He cheered her on in a soft voice.

"Lillian's gone." She laughed.

"Yeah, but the animals might hear."

"You're ridiculous." She slid her panties down and showed him just a little of what he wanted, loving the way his eyes lit up. Then she stretched the elastic waistband and let them zing away.

Charlie straddled him again. "I'm naked, you're not."

"This is interesting," he said, gazing at her with growing lust. "Where are you going with this?"

"Wouldn't you like to know."

She took her time with the buttons, sliding each one out of its buttonhole with a fingertip and then running both hands over his warm, T-shirted chest when the shirt was open. She circled her palms over each tight, hot little nipple and he practically purred.

"Nice," he murmured. "Yes. More."

Moving herself down to straddle his jeans-clad thighs, she leaned forward to stroke his taut belly, letting her bare breasts press ever so lightly against the huge bulge under his zipper.

Sam groaned. "Sweet torture. Can I move?"

"No. Not yet."

She rose halfway and played with her breasts as if no one was watching, not even looking at him for a minute. Then she did.

His eyes were on fire now. "You're going to

have to cuff me to this damn bed if I'm not allowed to touch you. No guarantees otherwise, Charlie."

She smiled and dropped forward on her hands and knees, covering his mouth with hers and kissing him deeply and passionately.

Sam's hands came up to fondle her breasts and tug pleasurably at her nipples. He captured her tiny moans in his mouth as she allowed him to get a little rougher and squeeze just fractionally harder. Mmm. It felt so good to her. Being apart a day and a half was really worthwhile.

She decided that tall worked lying down, too, when she felt his hands move from her breasts to her waist, and from there to her behind. Warmly and firmly, he caressed each cheek and pulled her down on him, so that she straddled his belly again, her breasts pressed comfortingly against the thin knit cotton of his T-shirt. They kissed for long minutes just like that, until he turned his head to the side to whisper in her ear.

"Enough of this. Let's both get naked."

Oh yeah. He still had his clothes on. Wriggling on top of him, completely bare but totally warm, she'd forgotten about that.

Charlie straightened, moving her knee over him to let him up but he caught it in midair and held her bent leg up. Slowly, very slowly, looking at her face, he slid a finger into the hot wetness that wasn't hidden anymore.

A little off balance and afraid to move, Charlie drew in her breath and let him do it, excited by the gentle, in-and-out sliding. He added another finger, still watching her face.

Charlie closed her eyes, not caring what he looked at, just enjoying herself. He withdrew his fingers and let her put her leg down, but he quickly found her clit and held it. With easy pressure, he excited that sensitive part of her, too, using little rubbing strokes that were so pleasurable she stayed exactly where she was to enjoy them. Her tumbled hair had fallen partly over her face, but she didn't brush it away.

"You're so beautiful," he murmured. "Every part of you is beautiful."

Charlie opened her eyes, feeling deeply aroused and dreamy, saying his name but not aloud.

He brought his exploring fingers to her lips, first pushing the hair away with the other hand, then placing his wet fingertips on her lower lip.

She obeyed the silent command to taste herself, and licked his fingers with just the tip of her tongue. Then she pulled his fingers into her mouth all at once, sucking tightly around them, swirling her tongue.

"Ohhh . . . yes." Sam blew out his breath. She let go and looked down at the bulge in his jeans. If she didn't undo that zipper right now, he was likely to go right through the frayed spot.

She moved aside and took the zipper tab in her fingers in about the same way he'd handled her clit and pulled it down little by little. Underneath it was more soft cotton and a very hard cock, straining up and out.

Charlie pushed down his briefs and took that into her mouth, feeling his whole body tense and arch slightly as she pleasured him. Licking her lips, she sat up when she felt him push down frantically on his confining jeans and briefs. In less than five seconds, he'd shucked all his clothes and was ready to return every favor.

"Lie on your back," he growled. She obliged, opening her legs and running her hands over the inside of her thighs. He watched for a second or two, that impressive erection standing out from his groin, then kneeled, burying his mouth in her damp curls and licking where his fingers had been, in and around, up and down.

As she began to writhe, he slid his hands under her behind and lifted her slightly to lick her better. Charlie gave a little cry and rested her legs on his broad back. She could feel him smile with satisfaction when she did. It made it easier for him to put his tongue in all the way.

Oh. Oh. Oh.

She couldn't resist the soft sensation and she came that way, in midair, held in his hands, her thighs clenching his head.

Charlie moaned, nearly sobbing with the intensely erotic feeling of this new position, as he let her down gently, wiping off his mouth when his hands were free.

He leaned over the bed and her, pressing her down into the mattress with the delicious weight of his body, looking for his bag and a condom. She didn't have to ask and he didn't say. Charlie felt the huge hot rod that was about to be sheathed against her thigh, then her soft belly, as he finally found what he was looking for and came back up.

This time he did the honors, ripping open the foil and unrolling the thin latex over himself with practiced speed. His hair hung over his forehead, shaggy with sweat and her ardent caresses as he looked down at himself for a second.

Then he looked at her.

"I can't decide," he muttered. "This way? On all fours? What do you want? Wow, you are so rosy. What a sex flush."

He dropped over Charlie on all fours and kissed her breasts and nipples with wild abandon, suckling her hard on one and then the other as he squeezed her breasts together.

She arched underneath him, moaning again, more excited than before.

"All fours," she whispered.

"What—mmf—yeah." His mouth was full when he replied but he let go quickly and rolled her around with one strong arm, positioning her with his hands.

Charlie buried her face in the pillow, loving the wanton quality of showing herself like this. He was stroking her all the way from her shoulders to down over her buttocks now, in long, warm slides that ended at the backs of her knees.

The sensation was soothing and extremely stimulating. Charlie couldn't help but respond, undulating in response to his touch, a sight that made him draw in his breath and . . . stop.

She knew what was coming and moaned for it, turning her head to one side on the crumpled pillow.

Sam positioned the heavy, sheathed head of his cock between her labia and didn't go any deeper. Just staying like that, he stroked her back and behind again. His movements were controlled and slow, but each caress did make his stiff rod move a little where it was.

She was going crazy with the anticipation of taking its full length deep inside her. But she let him tease her. That, too, was extremely pleasurable. His gentle strokes were a little less slow and not so careful as their mutual restraint excited them both, more and more.

Charlie was done waiting. She pushed backward, sliding herself over that huge, hot shaft to the hilt, making him cry out. Sam grabbed her hips and hung on, letting her set the pace until he couldn't stand it any longer.

He thrust the way he wanted to, hard and fast, then stopped all the way up inside her. She felt his big body drop over hers but he held himself up pretty well with all that middle muscle so he didn't weigh her down.

With his cock snugged up where it was, he supported himself with one hand and fondled her breasts with the other, careful to pay attention to both. His hand was big enough to hold both when he squeezed them together. He rocked inside her, letting go of her breasts and slapping them gently, then holding his palm flat so her erect, highly sensitive nipples brushed against it as her breasts swayed.

Charlie began to rock back, wanting everything he was doing to just keep on going, grateful she'd already had an orgasm so she could hold off for a little and let this one build inside her.

She felt his cock increase in circumference and remembered that he hadn't come. Above her, biting the back of her neck and still playing skillfully with her breasts and nipples, Sam was straining his taut hips against her behind. He didn't seem to want to give in to what had to be intensely erotic sensations for him as well.

Charlie smiled into the pillow and tightened her innermost muscles around him as she began to rotate her hips ever so slightly.

He reacted, big time. Sam grabbed her hips and held on tight as he rose up and thrust into her for all he was worth. She added a little clitoral stimulation for herself, playing with his balls while she was at it . . . until they tightened hard against his body.

They came together that time, loud and blissfully, and collapsed in a side by side heap. He flung one arm back over his head and scooped her to him with the other, his face glowing, his torso slick with fine sweat.

Dreamily, her body echoing with pleasure for the second time, Charlie nuzzled into him. "Welcome home," she said softly.

"Thanks," he gasped. "You sure know how."

And then they dozed off, not noticing the sunlight move through the room as the hours ticked away until afternoon.

She awoke with a start, realizing that he was no longer in the brass bed. Charlie sat up, hearing the faint clatter of pots and pans from the kitchen. Then she flopped back down and rolled herself up in the comforter, burying her nose in it because it smelled like him and her and great sex.

When he came into the room bearing a tray, she peeked at him over the top of it, her laughter muffled.

"Room service," he said.

"So I see." She folded the comforter down at an angle and gave him space to set down the tray. He wasn't wearing anything but jeans and his big feet were bare.

"Ma'am. You're naked. That's distracting. I'm only human and you're the most beautiful woman in this hotel." He put down the tray and stood there, his thumbs in the belt loops of his jeans.

"You're a peach," she said. "That looks fabulous and I'm starving."

With a flourish, he gestured to the meal for two on one big platter. Scrambled eggs, last night's steamed vegetables thrown around in a little sizzling butter, a stack of toast. OJ and coffee on the side. And, for a holiday touch, an iced gingerbread snowman who was missing most of his silver-ball buttons and his ribbon muffler—she remembered Gloria eating something ribbonlike last night and refusing to let go of it. Lillian had rescued the snowman, evidently.

She tucked into it while he watched and then he pushed over the tray and picked up a fork himself. He leaned over to kiss her mouth but missed, planting one an inch higher that made her laugh.

He grinned at her. "You have a good appetite and a cold nose. I think that means you're healthy."

"Mm-hm," she said, continuing to eat. "Speaking of that, how's your head? All better?"

"Now she asks," he groaned. "You didn't care when it was between your creamy thighs, did you? Noooo. All you could think about was—"

"Shut up," she said lovingly. "You do that so well, Sam. So incredibly well."

"I try to satisfy." He gave her a cocky grin.

She loved him like this. His natural wariness was gone, set aside somewhere or burned off by their shared sexual passion. "So did you finish the article?"

He nodded, tackling a slice of toast. "Yup. E-mailed it to Kevin late last night, complete with photos of a mystery blob and a picture of smoke that an innkeeper said was a weeping woman. I didn't think so. *Cherchez le bong,* I told her. What the hell. It's a paying gig."

"You didn't mention me in it, I hope."

He looked at her indignantly. "No way, Charlie. What do you take me for?"

She gave a delicate shrug. "A true professional."

That description made him grin. "Thanks. Kevin apparently thinks so, too. I sent him an alternate photo of the blob with a boobalicious blonde in a Santa hat." He held up a hand to forestall her inevitable who-was-she question. "Before you ask, she was a local girl who wanted to break into the big time. And she probably will, chest first. But I didn't touch her, believe me."

Great. He prided himself on being faithful for thirty-six hours. "Sorry. I'm just nervous, I guess."

He finished his bite and brushed the crumbs off his fingers onto the tray. "Everyone is, even in my business. Hard news doesn't sell, not that *Scoop* ever tried. But let's see which photo Kevin runs and where. I don't care. So what are you nervous about?"

"Everything, lately."

Sam pointed a finger at her but not rudely. "Break it down into bite-sized pieces. Then deal with them one at a time."

She thought that over.

"Which one bothers you the most?" Sam prodded gently.

Charlie didn't hesitate on the answer. "The ghosts, of course. I'd like to have a Christmas that's just you and me—" Whoops. She broke off at his impassive look. Had she said too much, expected too much? He'd promised her a few more days, if you could call that a promise. Nothing more.

"I was thinking about Christmas myself," he said calmly. "And you're right. Holidays are hard enough without supernatural beings carrying on in the spare room."

His tone was joking and light. Charlie smiled, trying to keep the mood on that level. She still didn't know him all that well, and the sexually intense chemistry they had wasn't necessarily helping that.

She wasn't sure whether this was the time to share what she'd learned about Temperance and Daniel either. A wayward daughter, an elopement on Christmas Eve that must have shattered her family, the storm that might have killed them both—it was too dramatic, too romantic.

What she and Sam had was nothing like that. It was basically so good and so downright good for them that it couldn't possibly be the product of a paranormal connection that neither of them understood.

It was real, and it felt like love. Having him so near after his short sojourn on the mainland emphasized that. It seemed to have done him good to take a breather. Once he'd gotten her safely tucked away at Lillian's, he'd been willing enough to leave. He sure seemed damn glad to be back.

Charlie smiled slightly, curling her toes with remembered pleasure. "I was a good girl," she told him. "I never once went over there."

He nodded approvingly. "So what did you do?"

"Hung out with Lillian. Walked around town some. She took me to the town archives," she said offhandedly.

"Yeah?" His ears practically pricked up. "Find out anything about the Prescott ghosts?"

"We didn't have a chance to go through all the

boxes," she said noncommittally. "But there were some interesting things in a few. Documents. Tintypes. And other stuff." She didn't mention the diary, determined to save that for another time that was closer to everyday reality and didn't include mind-bendingly passionate sex. The two didn't mix. "We're going to go back. Want to come along?"

"Sure," he said. "I actually do like research. Plus the Prescotts are truly freaky, underneath their mild-mannered exteriors." He winked at her.

"We are not," she replied, not too convincingly.

He blew her a kiss. "But I like you that way. No one ever gave me any prizes for normalcy either." He changed the subject. "How's Butch doing?"

"He likes it here and he sleeps on top of Gloria. She doesn't seem to mind."

Sam picked up the platter and finished up all the food. "Must be love," he said, setting it down.

"I think it's more like a mutual non-aggression pact, actually."

He lifted the tray off the bed and let her take her cup of coffee before he set it on the floor. "Whatever works. So—let me know when you want to go back home. If you still think of the Prescott place as home."

"I do." Charlie took a few sips. "I'd rather go with you, though. After you've rested."

He thumped his chest in a weak imitation of Tarzan. "Give me another twenty-four hours."

"Take all the time you want. I'm still afraid that you're a target somehow."

He shook his head before he leaned back into a pile of pillows. "Maybe. Maybe not. The ghost didn't attack me that last time in the kitchen, you know."

"What? C'mon, Sam, I saw the blood. You were unconscious for a little while, too. What are you talking about?"

He looked at her a little sheepishly. "I—ah—sorta threw myself backward into the cabinets. Didn't work out quite the way I planned."

"What?" She stared at him incredulously.

"I did. Granted, I didn't think before I did it that it actually was possible to knock yourself out. But, being a guy, I proved myself wrong."

Charlie set the cup to one side. "You did that to get me to come here to Lillian's house?"

He nodded. "Am I brilliant or what?"

"I feel really guilty." She laughed. "I would have given in eventually."

"Nah. You weren't going to budge and I wasn't up for more arguing. So . . . boom."

"Oh, Sam—"

"I couldn't protect you if I wasn't there, right? So it made sense. At the time."

"You're crazy." Charlie wiggled closer to him, running her hands through his hair and checking for—exactly what, she wasn't sure. Blood. Swelling.

"Thanks, nurse," he whispered lasciviously.

"Why?"

"B'ful bouncin' boobs 'n my face." He'd latched onto a nipple. "Cures ever'fin.'"

Charlie laughed and detached herself carefully. "You seem to be all right."

He looked bereft. "No. I need another treatment. Just like that. Don't ever get dressed, okay? I want you in a big bed like this one for—"

Her breath caught for a second and he gave her a worried look. What had he been about to say? Forever. For now. *Oh, forget it,* she told herself. *He's just being playful and you don't have to take every minute you spend with him so seriously.* She smiled at him. "Dibs on the shower. I'm getting up."

He groaned, grabbing at her, but she eluded him. "Can I watch?" she heard him call over the running water.

"If you want to."

She was under the warm, pulsing stream by the time he came. He swished the vinyl curtain partly aside just as she was blinking and wondering where the soap was.

In his hand.

"Allow me," he murmured suavely.

Charlie gave him a dripping grin and turned around slowly, letting him do the honors. He seemed awfully happy to take it slow, washing her with both hands, squeezing out suds between his fingers as they slid over her skin, bending her over for an intimate and very tender wash when he'd finished with her from the waist up.

He threw down the bathmat and kneeled on it to lean in and soap her legs with worshipful, long strokes from thighs to ankles. The shower's spray was getting his hair wet but he didn't seem to care. The front of his jeans were wet, too, where they were pressing against the bathtub.

His fingers circled her ankle and she braced herself as he lifted her foot, and lavished attention on her toes. He did the other, then sat back on his haunches with a satisfied sigh, letting her rinse off while he just drank in the sight.

There was no missing his lusty grin or his huge hard-on, bigger than before.

"Look at you. Aren't you uncomfortable in those wet jeans?" she said. Charlie squirted shampoo from a plastic cylinder into her cupped palm as she talked, rubbing it into her drenched hair.

His eyes tracked her breasts with boundless appreciation as they lifted and jiggled while she shampooed. He kept right on staring as he stood up, peeled off the jeans with some difficulty. Then he leaned forward to lick drops of water from her erect nipples, the shower spray bouncing off his back now.

She closed her eyes, letting the water sluice away the last of the shampoo. Getting clean and getting licked at the same time was a very nice feeling. In another few seconds, Sam's big naked body was next to hers in the shower, and he was hugging her, sliding his body against hers in a tight caress. He turned so that she turned, leaving her standing under the pulsing shower, then kneeling himself in the other part of the tub.

Knowingly, Charlie stepped her feet a little apart, then reached down and opened herself for him with her fingers. Again he applied his magic tongue to her most sensitive flesh, giving her a squeaky-clean orgasm in a minute, then struggling up to kiss her and caress her all over.

She returned the favor with her hand and the soft soap, and he got off in seconds, spurting hotly over her circling fingers as he moaned against her wet hair, gripping her shoulders to keep his balance.

They stood there for a little while, letting the wonderful feelings swirl and ebb around their gleaming bodies, and then she shut off the spray.

He threw his head back and for a moment she thought he was going to roar. But he didn't—he was just shaking his hair to get some of the water out, getting drops in her face.

"Silly—step out and I'll towel you off," she said.

"Only if you let me do the same to you."

She had to laugh. "Deal."

The soft, dry scrubbing he gave her was nearly as pleasurable as the rest. God, she thought, as he used a corner to even dry the whorls in her outer ears, getting spectacularly laid and loved up and pampered to the max had a way of making meaningless worries disappear. A lot of things that had been on her mind just weren't anymore. She struggled to remember what they were—oh yes. Had the ghosts inspired them and was he capable of commitment and how did you know when love was real? Those things. Why couldn't she think? Because he'd wrapped the towel sarong-style around her bare ass and was rubbing it briskly back and forth.

"You have to go away more," she said when she stopped laughing. "It's so great when you come back."

"Whatever you say," Sam murmured, pulling her to him with the towel. "That really could work, you know."

Chapter Sixteen

Charlie opened the front door to the Prescott house—her house, she reminded herself—and lingered on the doorsill. The air was still and warm. She'd left the heat on and too many lights. Maybe it was kind of ridiculous to think that a package of 75-watt bulbs could keep supernatural emanations at bay, but it was no more ridiculous than garlic for werewolves.

Feeling a tad braver, she went inside. Sam came up the stairs behind her. "Wait for me," he called from the sidewalk.

"I did. I got bored," she called back.

His booted tread echoed in the quiet house once he was through the door and had shut it behind him.

"Everything looks about the same," he said.

"You get to check out the spare room."

Sam nodded resolutely. She was beginning to realize that he got off on being a hero, so long as he could wear his regular clothes: jeans, flannel shirt, boots, and parka. He thundered up the stairs. "Gotta let them know I'm coming," he said over his shoulder to her.

"Sounds like a plan." Charlie stood at the bottom of the stairs and waited. She never would've gone above the first floor if he hadn't been with her. She listened to the floorboards creak, judging his location by the sound.

He seemed to be opening and shutting doors more noisily than was necessary. She was aware that he'd also looked into the room where her computer was. Good. She didn't even want to switch that on unless he was standing right behind her.

To do what? she wondered. Smash a clenched fist through the monitor if the ghosts got frisky and put on an X-rated show in it? Charlie smiled a little. Nothing could be better than the incredible sensuality of her hours alone with Sam. She looked up as he came back down the stairs. "Everything looks okay. But I still think you should stay out of the spare room."

"Fine with me," she agreed.

He gave her an appraising onceover. "Are you going to be okay by yourself?"

"Sam, you can't babysit me. And I—we—can't stay at Lillian's indefinitely. Besides . . ." She hesitated.

"What?"

"Don't you have a place of your own to go back to?"

"Well, yeah. I sublet a place in Roxbury that

belongs to a buddy of mine. But there's nothing in it that I have to worry about. I don't own anything worth stealing and I rent cars. It's just me and my laptop, on the go. No kittycat. No fish tank. No plant, not even moss."

She bit her lip. "So you really are a rolling stone."

"Guess so," he said. "But don't look at me like it's a character failing. For the work I do, it's how I have to live. Not everyone gets to inherit an oceanfront house on Martha's Vineyard, you know."

His tone wasn't sarcastic, just honest, but the remark still stung a little. Still, she had no right to judge how he lived and it was obvious he wasn't attached to his apartment in any way, wherever it was.

"Right. Sorry if I sounded nosy."

He kissed her on that part of her face. "But it's a cute one."

Sam walked through the downstairs room with even more energy. His stride was restless and his eyes were everywhere.

"What are you looking for?" she asked him.

"Not really anything. I was just thinking that the house could use a little, you know, Christmas cheer."

"I keep trying to mull wine with spices and orange peel," she said. "No one seems interested."

"I didn't mean the kind of cheer that comes in a bottle. I was thinking"—he waved his arm at the living room—"that you could get a pretty big tree in here. If you wanted to."

"You mean like a Christmas tree?"

"No, a giant sequoia. Knock out the ceiling, knock out the floor. There's plenty of room. Make a statement."

He hugged her when she finally realized he was kidding—but not about the Christmas tree.

"I don't have any decorations, Sam."

"There must be some around here in boxes."

She pressed her lips together and shook her head. "Uh-uh. I'm not poking through old stuff or crawling around in attics."

"Okay, then we can go to one of those cute little Edgartown shops and buy new stuff. What do you say?"

Charlie thought it over. "Sure. We can pick up a tree stand at the hardware store and they probably have lights, too."

"I draw the line at stringing cranberries," he warned her. "I may be a New Englander, but I just don't get what's so freaking great about cranberries, and I mean eating them or anything else."

"Lillian would be shocked to hear that, but I don't care. But before we go, one more thing—"

"Say the word, Charlie."

She took him by the hand. "Go upstairs with me and open all the doors. Show me there's nothing there. And boot up my computer for me."

"Not a problem." He gave her hand a warm squeeze and led the way.

It was fun wandering around the hardware store and especially the shops, picking out ornaments. The selection was heavy on whales but what could you do. She chose glass bead garlands that looked easy to string, even for a couple of newbie tree-decorators like her and Sam.

She purchased clothespin dolls that were locally made and he picked out glass birds with shimmering tails. They both agreed on plain colored balls in assorted colors to fill out the bare spots and filled up a sailbag with it all, then went to Ed's lot to pick out a tree.

Ed was a giant of a man, with a huge belly and a mustache trimmed with frost. He reminded her a lot of a walrus, especially when he slapped his giant nylon mittens together to keep his circulation going. She almost expected him to make that orking noise, and smiled at his blunt greeting.

"Hiya. Those just came in." He waved a flipper—nylon mitten—at a row of tied-up pines with pointy, trembling tops.

"Thanks," Sam said. "We'll check 'em out."

This felt so . . . normal, she thought wonderingly. And nice. All she was doing was hanging on to Sam's parka-clad arm, aware of the warm muscle underneath, and strolling up and down the rows of dark, deliciously fragrant pine trees, cut so recently that their trunks still oozed fresh sap.

"We have to pick the best one," he told her. "And remember, there is only *one* best one. So take your time."

Ed was busy with someone else and it didn't matter if they took forever. Charlie was content.

She nudged him and pointed. "How about that one?"

"Perfect," he said.

"You didn't even look at it, Sam!"

"If you want it, then it's perfect," he said firmly.

This really could work, she thought to herself.

Ed dropped off the tree an hour later, pulling it out of the back of his truck and going back to the lot. It was getting closer to Christmas and business had picked up in the evening after they'd left.

Sam lugged it over the doorsill and plunked it down on the carpet.

"Not there," she said.

"It's going in the living room, right?"

"Yes. In a tree stand. You're going to get the carpet full of needles and they'll never come out."

Sam made an exasperated noise and picked up the tree, throwing it over his shoulder. "Then where do you want it? In the bathtub?"

She realized she was being a trippy little fussbudget and ran to get the tree stand, putting it in the corner. "Bring it on," she said.

Sam came over and held the trunk an inch over the positioning screws while she guided it down. "Does this remind you of anything?" he asked, spitting out a few pine needles with even less regard for the carpet than he'd shown before. But she was more forgiving, because eating tree wasn't an improvement over eating humble pie.

"No, not at all," she said innocently. "Okay, hold it there. An inch off the bottom now so it can get the water."

"It's officially dead, you know. The process of water uptake by capillary action and osmosis is no longer operative."

"Is that going to be on the midterm? Is the tree straight? I can't see from down here."

"No," he answered. "And yes to the second question. But I can't see either. I'm dancing cheek to cheek with it."

"Check when you step back. I almost have it. So why do they sell tree stands with reservoirs?" She turned the thick screws evenly on all sides.

"You done?"

"Yes."

He stepped away from it. "Because it makes people feel better about cutting down trees," he replied. He put his hands on his hips. "Hey, how about that—you got it right the first time. It's perfectly straight."

She crawled out from under. "Really? Not bad. Considering how bent we are."

He extended a hand and pulled her up. "Good work, Charlie. Is this your first all-by-yourself tree?"

She nodded, looking at it with pride and rubbing a trace of sticky sap between her fingers. "Let's decorate this baby."

Sam went to get the sailbag with the ornaments. "Got any libations?"

"I could make fresh eggnog," she answered from the kitchen.

"Too much work. Fake is fine."

"Okay." She opened the fridge and reached for

the unopened quart behind the almost empty one. It was a second before she realized that it was not only open—the top had been carefully pinched to look like it wasn't but almost empty, too.

Guess who. She was suddenly sure it was Daniel—just touching the eggnog carton had brought back her feeling that he hadn't been anything like the sober New Englanders around here. She could probably add *bon vivant* and *mooch* to the word *dandy* to describe him. Maybe even *con man*.

She took out both eggnog cartons, throwing them in the trash, noticing that she sensed nothing about Temperance from them and she now knew what Temperance looked like.

Beautiful. Passionate. And undoubtedly genuinely innocent as well. Maybe Daniel had introduced her to worldly pleasures. Maybe Cyrus Prescott hadn't been wrong.

She stood stock still for a minute, her eyes closed, trying to sense something, anything about the female half of their ghostly visitors. In the vaguest possible way, she received a vibration that Temperance was all right. Somehow.

Charlie opened her eyes, feeling a little silly.

"Sorry. Looks like I'm out," she called brightly. So Daniel had been raiding the refrigerator in her absence—and what was it with him and eggnog? Charlie thought to check the whiskey—that bottle was down to an inch or less.

"What else do you have?"

She pondered telling him about the midnight

raid on the liquor—as usual, she somehow couldn't imagine the culprit doing his worst in the day, and decided against it. She was not going to get hysterical or let the past interfere with the present. And that was that.

"How about a gin and tonic?" she called to Sam.

"God, I haven't had one of those for years. I used to drink them in the summer, though."

"They're good any time, very refreshing."

"Okay."

Charlie went to the other cabinet and opened the door. Lillian liked a gin and tonic now and then, which was why she had the makings of them. The familiar green tank-style jug was full and none of the small tonics had been taken—there was a complete six-pack of squat, yellow-labeled bottles. Okay. So Daniel didn't like gin or hadn't found it.

Charlie went to the fruit bowl on the table and took out a lime to slice into quarters. She squeezed one in a glass for juicy flavor to counteract the tonic's bitterness, and adding another for garnish when she'd put in the ice and the gin, finishing off with the bubbly tonic so as not to flatten it.

"Here you go," she said, coming back into the living room. In her absence, Sam had managed to decorate exactly half of the tree with half of the ornaments.

"Thanks, babe. You can do the rest."

She smiled. "What about the lights? Aren't they supposed to go on first?"

He sipped his drink about halfway. "Wooah.

Cold and strong. Yes, you're right. Okay, I'll take everything off and we can start again."

Charlie twined her arms around his waist. "You're like a little kid. Happy all over because Christmas is coming and nothing could go wrong."

He handed her the rest of the drink and eased out of her hold, intent on his task. "On the contrary. I know everything can go wrong. It's that I just don't care."

Charlie sipped at the gin and tonic, glad that it was diluted a bit by the melting ice cubes, whose corners had rounded down. "Explain. I'm not sure I understand."

He was unhooking the ornaments and putting them in a neat row on the coffee table. "I did a lot of thinking on the way back."

"About what?"

"Life. Us. The big stuff."

Charlie swallowed a largish piece of ice by accident and waited for it to slide down to her stomach, feeling a weird but not unpleasant chill. "Oh," she said after a little while. "Um, what conclusions did you come to?"

"That everything generally works out okay if you have a few good people in your life. And your health. And something you love to do, even if you don't do it for a living. It really is that simple."

"God, I hope so," she said fervently.

"It was the blob that really got me thinking."

"The blob," she repeated. "Is that like—your new religion? Blobism?"

"No." He laughed. "I just felt so damn ridiculous standing there and poking it and taking pictures of it, and later, I started to think. Kevin can fire me—I'll land another gig."

"I'm sure you can."

"And then I started thinking about you."

Uh-oh. She didn't say anything, just looked at him with what she knew were sad-puppy eyes.

"I couldn't wait to get back to you," he said. "I just wanted to lie next to you, talk to you, hear what you had to say, cuddle you all night long if you wanted me to—"

"Sure," she said, her tension easing. "Sign me up."

"Then I got that scary feeling men get when things get real, though. Fair warning."

"Okay," she said, her voice measured. "Then what?"

"I talked myself out of it. Since we started doing one thing spectacularly right and that would be the fantastic sex, I figured we had a good shot at the rest."

"The rest. Meaning—"

"Um, a relationship?" he said, rubbing the back of his neck and looking at her worriedly.

"Oh, one of those. Of course." She thought briefly of the previous candidates, Guys #1, #2, #3, and #4. "For a second, I wasn't sure what you were getting at, Sam." Part of her was elated and part of her was as uneasy as he still seemed to be.

"You know, you and me, for a while," he said helpfully. "Just us. Together."

"Right."

"You don't sound thrilled, Charlie."

"I'm thinking."

He put his hand to his chin and pondered the tree. "Go right ahead. I did kind of rush at you with this, didn't I?"

"Rushing can be good," she pointed out. "You rushed me into bed and that worked out great. Fools rush in to lots of things and no one ever stops them. So let's take—the rest, if you want to call it that—one day at a time."

"That's what I was hoping you'd say. Words to that effect, anyway. And it'll work out. If it doesn't, you can kick me to the curb—I'll go back to my Roxbury place. Life goes on, whether we want it to or not."

"That's deep."

He finished removing the ornaments. "Ready to do the lights?"

"Sure."

"I'm not saying that I expect to be kicked to the curb," he said. "Just that I realized I would be okay if you did. And that made me less scared."

"You? Scared?" She was joking but she did understand what he was getting at. They had shared the most glorious physical experiences of her life. "The rest" didn't seem as easy to her, either.

But right now they had a tree to decorate. And she wanted it to work out fine. Charlie picked out a clothespin doll and stuck it on a pine twig. It leaned way over to the side, looking a little scared itself.

"The lights," he reminded her.

"I almost forgot." She took off the clothespin

and went to get them, handing him one end as she unspooled them from the package insert. He started at the top and she fed him the green wire, plugging in the next strand to it when they ran out around the middle.

Charlie had to crawl under the tree when they'd gotten all the lights on to plug in the end of the last strand and she fumbled it. Sam got down on hands and knees to help her. His long arms made the reach and he popped the plug in, looking at her through the spindly bottom branches when the tree lit up above them.

"Hey," he said softly. "Did I explain myself at all?"

"You kind of did. And I think I get it," she answered honestly. "Anyway, Christmas is coming. One day at a time sounds like a good idea. Holidays are weird." She backed out and he did the same.

Both of them heard a noise from upstairs. A scrabbling sound, followed by a jump.

"Goddamn it," he said crossly, looking up at the ceiling while he sat on his haunches. "Are they back?"

Charlie got up, brushing pine needles out of her hair. "I don't think they ever went away."

"What do you want me to do?" he asked resignedly.

"Go up there and look around. Call me when it's safe to come up. Does that sound fair?"

He nodded and scrambled to his feet. "In other words, be your hero."

"Yes. If you don't mind."

Sam gave her a world-class grin. "I think I'm getting the hang of it, Charlie. Grab the poker and wait at the bottom of the stairs."

"Deal," she said.

A few minutes later, she was listening to him moving stealthily overhead. Something fell, he thudded against a wall, and her knuckles turned white around the black iron handle of the poker.

"Gotcha!" he cried.

Charlie's eyes widened. He couldn't actually have caught a ghost. They were invisible. Elusive. And unpredictable. She heard the steady sound of his footsteps next and got ready to whack— Daniel, she hoped. And she also hoped that she wouldn't whack Sam by accident.

He was looking down at her, a very relaxed Butch in his arms. "It was the cat."

"How did he get in?" She set down the poker and went halfway up the stairs.

Sam shrugged, stroking his ears and rubbing his head until Butch emitted a faint but blissful purr. "He must have dashed in when we came in. Cats are real homebodies."

"Butchie," she cooed to him, accompanying the two of them back down to the first floor, "you wanted to be home, didn't you? With me . . ."

Butch, the betrayer, looked adoringly up at the man who was carrying him.

". . . and Sam," she added.

The cat purred loudly and settled back down inside those strong arms.

"You have five minutes more," she told the cat and rubbed his head. "Then I get him back. We have to finish the tree, okay?"

But she let Sam hold him and watch while she did the rest. Five minutes, thirty minutes. So long as her two guys were happy. Plus, she got to do the decorating her way.

Later that night, curled up with just Sam, the cat opting for a spot underneath the prickly, fragrant tree downstairs, she woke up in the wee hours and knew she wouldn't be able to get back to sleep. She eased herself away from him and got up quietly, looking for a robe.

Charlie wrapped it around herself and blew him a silent kiss.

Charlie sat down at her computer, hitching her robe up so she was comfortable and clicking absentmindedly on the mouse to get her e-mail from BlinkLink, the world's cheesiest Internet service provider on the planet. She was surprised, in fact, that it wasn't their official slogan. Scrolling through after the site appeared and she'd clicked to open her inbox, she didn't look too closely at any of it because she didn't notice anything new in boldface type.

Wait. There was one from Pages, which was Lillian's work e-addy. Charlie clicked it open.

Called my house, no answer. You and Sam must have gone home.

It was signed with a winking emoticon and an uppercase L.

Charlie typed back.

Yes we did! See you tomorrow!

She signed her brief answer with a beaming sun face, not finding an emoticon for we-had-glorious-sex-all-afternoon-and-we-seem-to-be-talking-about-falling-in-love. Especially since the glorious sex had been had in Lillian's house and saying so just seemed weird, even though Lillian probably wouldn't care in the least. And saying anything about falling in love would trigger a barrage of questions Charlie had no idea how to answer at the moment.

The rest of the new messages were just come-ons but at least she knew they were generated by companies she bought stuff from online. No spam, thank goodness. It might be a fact of modern life but it still annoyed the hell out of her. She didn't bother to sign out, just minimized the box so it appeared in the bottom frame of the screen.

Charlie stifled a yawn, hoping to cure her insomnia by going to the most boring Web sites she knew. Which meant no Stephen Colbert, no Huffington Post, no Perez Hilton. She tried *One Thousand and One Home Repairs* but actually found that sort of interesting and clicked out. *Fishing Fundamentals* did the trick. A few minutes of watching two thick-necked guys in an aluminum boat on some anonymous lake and she was definitely drowsy.

Charlie rubbed her eyes, shifting in her chair to

take in a few more soporific moments of Milt and Spawn, or whatever their names were, chatting about some monster muskie they were after. Then the monitor shimmered and the fishermen disappeared. Oh hell.

Was the monitor on the fritz? The computer was working fine, but she hadn't bought them at the same time. The monitor was older—it had never given her any trouble, though. She didn't have enough money to buy a new monitor right now. Charlie peered into it, wondering if it was her sleepiness or a trick of the low light or a malfunction that was making her see things.

Vague shapes. Could be people. Could be dogs. They had heads, anyway.

Then the shapes faded away and she watched letters, rapidly typed, form words and then sentences. Coherent sentences.

Charlie sat up very straight.

A most ingenious machine, this. Better than any of my magic contraptions. Hello, Charlotte. This is Daniel.

She stared at the message, then typed a reply.

Go away.

She could almost swear she heard ghostly laughter, but she didn't trust her ears. Or her eyes. Was Sam pulling her leg? Couldn't be. She had left him snoring peacefully and she could still just barely hear the steady rumble from his manly chest.

Another answer popped up on her screen. From then on, the exchange between her and

the being who called himself Daniel was fast
and furious.

Why should I go away? I live here, off and on.

—How did you get into my house? And my
computer?

**The house first, if you please. It was easy. I
walked in through the front door a day after
you arrived in Edgartown. I had been drifting
around for a while, unseen. You have a well-
stocked liquor cabinet, my dear Charlotte,
which you hardly touch. Alas, I have a regret-
table weakness for drink.**

—I noticed that. Go away. I insist.

She thought for a minute, then added something.

—Is there just one of you?

**Ah, you know about Temperance. I was
never worthy of her.**

—What do you mean?

**I seduced her. She convinced herself that
she was madly in love with me and agreed
to elope.**

—When?

Charlie waited in breathless disbelief for the
answer to that question, reminding herself that
she was the only person alive who knew the ap-
proximate date. Lillian hadn't read much of
the old diary or so she'd said. That left only her
friend Iris Munson and Charlie hadn't had the
impression that Iris had read it at all.

On Christmas Eve.

She rocked back in her chair, her hands covering her mouth. She had to keep him talking. This had to be Daniel. Only he or Temperance would know that. Or—

Her sister Constance was the only one who knew of our clandestine affair. Dear girl. She helped us run away.

—In the middle of winter?

Not the wisest decision, was it? A tremendous blizzard hit that very night and raged for days. Mr. and Mrs. Prescott undoubtedly assumed we had died in it.

—Did you?

No. We had reached an inn on the mainland.

—Then where did you go?

We traveled through Massachusetts to New York. For a while, I was able to keep Temperance in splendid accommodations worthy of her beauty. Our bedroom was done up in fine red velvet, you know. We had to sell it all for pennies on the dollar after a few years in New York.

—Did you ever marry her?

No. After a while she did not want me to. I think she hoped to return to Edgartown eventually, but she was loyal to me in her way. She used to hide the whiskey from me.

—I don't doubt it.

Well, that is the Prescott in you. Hiding things. Judging other people.

—How dare you talk to me like that?

I have never lacked for nerve. Cyrus Prescott always said I was a bounder and a cad. He was right.

Charlie hardly knew what to say or how much to believe of the incredible things she was reading. For sure no one would ever believe her if she told anyone. Their back-and-forth had the creepy intimacy of a chat room exchange and a musty whiff of yesteryear. Her mind felt overwhelmed and under pressure, as if the ghost had somehow gotten inside it or could read her thoughts. She had no way of knowing if either was true. Frantically, she tapped the function keys that were meant to automatically save e-mails or anything that appeared on the monitor but they seemed to be stuck.

Don't bother. I have been playing with your keyboard in my idle hours. Then I slipped inside the monitor. As a wraith, I can do such things. A computer is a most ingenious contraption.

Reading that infuriated Charlie. Doing it was bad enough. How dare he brag about it? She lost her temper and hit the Cap Lock button.

—**WHO ARE YOU REALLY????????????**
Do not shout.
—**WHAT DO YOU WANT????????**
Just to chat. I find I am lonely. Being a ghost is less interesting than I thought it would be.

Charlie took a deep breath and let it out slowly. She composed her thoughts before her fingers touched the keyboard again.

—**Tell me everything. Who you are, what you did. I find you fascinating.**

That stuck in her craw, but he might feel flattered.

I? It has been a while since anyone has asked that question. I was a jack of all trades, I suppose. Mostly dishonest ones. I wrote fictional accounts of ghastly crimes for the penny papers, for one.

—Writing doesn't pay.

She hit the period key hard to emphasize that.

It did if a high-ranking official or society swell wished not to be mentioned in connection with murder. I made all of that up, but it didn't matter. Scandal is a lucrative business when it is managed right.

—Oh.

And I performed magic shows at private parties so I could pick pockets or simply charm wealthy women out of their baubles. I invented quite a few ingenious devices of my own to assist me in that endeavor.

—I see. What were you doing in Edgartown?

I was an advance man for a circus. I smoothed the way with the leading citizens so that we might be allowed to set up our tents. On the outskirts of town, of course. But my salary permitted me to stay in the best available inn and keep the sawdust off my shoes.

—How did you meet Temperance?

She mistook me for a man of means, well-educated and well-placed in society. I was quite good at impressions of all sorts.

—You took advantage of her.

There was a pause of several moments before
he replied.

**You are indeed shrewd, Charlotte. But it
could also be true that she took advantage of
me. I seemed like a way out, you see. Even a
beautiful woman could not go far without
male protection and she knew that.**

—She was beautiful. I saw her tintype.

Another pause.

Where?

It was the only question he'd asked with a single
word. He'd tipped his hand. Charlie wasn't going
to answer him. If the past was going to stay past,
Daniel couldn't be rummaging through the historical society archives because he had nothing
better to do. It occurred to her that he might turn
the house upside down looking for the tintype if
he thought it was there.

—**Never mind. She looked intelligent but
also innocent.**

**Your comment is accurate. Her passionate
nature was her undoing. And once she had
fled with me, she was a ruined woman for all
intents and purposes. But eventually she lived
up to her name. Dear Temperance. She de-
tested my drinking, tried to cure me of it because I got into brawls so often. I remember
her dragging me out of a saloon by the collar
of my coat. I found the sidewalk cruelly hard
when she dropped me upon it.**

—**Good for her. And shame on you. I feel
sorry for her.**

Ah, well. She wanted to see the world. She did see some of it.

—And what happened to her? You still haven't told me that.

No? The ending is an anticlimax, I'm afraid. She grew older, her beauty vanished, we had no children, her family had long since disowned her—the usual story. But she never did leave me.

So there was no happy ending. Well, Charlie hadn't expected one. But at least Temperance had a few years of luxury and a taste of freedom for a while. Maybe that was all a woman of her day could hope for.

—Is that her I see sometimes? Naked?

You are bold, Charlotte, to ask such a question. Yes, that is her, when she was young. But what you see is my memory of her. She faded away into nothingness.

—And how do you stay in this world?

I drink far too much. But I suspect that the alcohol preserves me. Ha ha.

—I think it makes you behave badly. You tried to rough up Sam.

So I did. It takes enormous effort for a ghost to do that. But I underestimated my remaining strength—or your whiskey. It has a potent effect on a soused spirit, you see.

Charlie was both appalled and fascinated by the supernatural exchange and didn't look up when Sam padded into the room. He cleared his throat and she jumped in her chair.

"Oh God. You startled me."

"Sorry. What are you doing?" he asked calmly. "Checking your e-mail?"

"Yes. You're not going to believe this—"

"Whatever it is can wait. C'mon back to bed." He reached out his hand.

Charlie shook her head. "Look over my shoulder. I can't save this and it may disappear forever. You have to read this."

His forehead creased with a sleepy frown and he scrubbed at his face to make himself wake up a little more. "Charlie—"

"I mean it," she said urgently. "Read this!"

He came around in back of her, leaning over her head with his hands on the back of her chair. "Are you writing this? I don't understand."

"No, no, this isn't like that book that just— appeared. This is Daniel, writing directly to me."

"Who is he again?"

"The lover in the story and in real life, long ago. But I think he got into my computer and somehow tricked me into writing about him and Temperance."

"Your long-lost, great-something Temperance?"

"Yes!" She scrolled up to the beginning, her hand on the mouse, feeling his hand cover hers when she reached the first line of the exchange and take over for the scrolling down.

The monitor in its altered state cast a gray light on his face as he read, his expression increasingly serious. He came to the last line from Daniel and looked down at her.

"Was your e-mail account up on the screen when he contacted you?"

"Yes. Why?"

"Close it out. Cancel it. Now."

"But—"

He straightened, folding his arms across his robed chest. "Just do it, Charlie. Before Daniel figures out some other way to get inside your head."

"Okay. I hope he can't hear us."

Sam blew out his breath. "I don't think so. Right now I'm pretty sure we've got the genie in a bottle and I'd like to keep him there."

"You mean he's actually inside my computer?"

"The monitor, definitely. I'm not sure about the computer. But if he travels via electrical energy, he could move from one to the other. Any other peripherals connected to it? Printer? Hard drive?"

"No."

More of Daniel's prattle was appearing on the screen.

"Don't stop to read it. Do what I said. Pull up the e-mail account and cancel it. He may end up in a giant global server somewhere but you'll be rid of him. Let their IT guys deal with it. They've seen worse."

Charlie clicked into this and out of that, and checked every box that made sense to her, working fast, knowing that Daniel's ghost was underneath what she'd pulled up.

Talking away. Expecting an answer.

She checked the last box marked Cancel All and signed herself out for the last time.

The gray blurriness vanished and a blue screen took its place. Across it scrolled a final message.

Fortunately, it was from BlinkLink, which provided her e-mail service and besieged her with endless ads into the bargain. *Dear Valued Customer* . . .

She didn't bother to read the rest of their sayonara form letter.

"Done." She twirled in her chair and looked up worriedly at Sam. "Do you really think we trapped him?"

The screen was flickering again.

"Shut the computer down," Sam said. "He is in it. Now!"

Another couple of clicks and that, too, was done. She unplugged the entire setup for good measure as he nodded his approval.

"Now what?" she asked.

"We wait and see. If he doesn't come back, then it worked. But you are going to need a new computer. And this one is going to have its hard drive extracted and melted down by a geek I know just in case."

"I can't afford a new computer!"

"Guess what? Kevin liked the article. I was just checking my e-mail, too. He's going to run the blob and the blonde on the front page and he's shooting me a bonus check that will cover it, plus allow me to take a month off until January to be with you."

He smiled down at her. "Christmas is coming. Ho ho ho. I think I solved your ghost problem."

"You said we'd have to wait and see."

Sam grinned and swept her up in his arms. "Just in case I'm right, you can thank me in advance."

"Oh—" She tried a few cute protesting kicks and then she settled down, digging the experience. "All right. I can see why Butch was so into this. Being carried around is great."

"Shhh." He maneuvered her through the door. "We're in my house, remember? Who's listening?"

He got her down the hall and through the bedroom door and they stayed up for the rest of the night talking about everything under the sun, bathed in moonlight all the while.

Chapter Seventeen

The next day saw Charlie back at Pages, helping Lillian with inventory and generally making herself useful. The older woman looked a bit frazzled, her pewter-colored hair spiking every which way, and Charlie felt a little guilty for not helping her more when Lillian had been the best neighbor in the world.

When she was not lugging cartons of books and Lillian wasn't seeing to the occasional customer, she filled her in on the events of last night. Lillian listened with wide eyes.

"So that's what happened to Temperance. Oh, my. Not a happy ending, was it?"

"No," Charlie said. "But that part of Daniel's story sounded real. It was hard to tell what he was making up and what could have been true. All I had to go on was what I read of that old diary, and you and I weren't in the archives for very long."

"Do you want to go back?"

Charlie shook her head firmly. "No."

Lillian gave a wistful sigh. "But what a story. You could write it, you know."

"I'd rather not. Let Temperance rest. I got the idea she was a bit of a drama queen, so she probably would prefer if no one knew what happened. Exit, stage left, amidst a howling blizzard. Way to go, right?"

"I guess so."

Charlie's tone was a lot more firm than Lillian's. "If anyone else looks into that box and reads her sister's diary, Temperance will be remembered as a strong-willed beauty who vanished with her lover. Where did she go? What happened? No one knows."

"I love plots like that. They sell," Lillian said regretfully.

"Hey, you can write it. That material is in the public domain."

Lillian shook her head, and her silver chandelier earrings tinkled faintly. "No. She's your long-lost relative, not mine. I just wouldn't."

"Thanks, Lillian." They both watched a customer come in and go straight to his favorite section, natural history. He took out a book on New England and began to peruse it.

"So far there's been no sign of Daniel anywhere in the house. We sat in the spare room. That strange heat didn't come back and Sam didn't get touched. Except by me," she said cheerfully, "later and somewhere else. I still don't like that room."

"What about your computer?"

"It's not only unplugged, I cut the cord so no one can start it up, even by accident. Sam knows a guy who can destroy the hard drive and that's the end of that. We hope," she added.

"So you actually talked to Daniel."

Charlie shuddered. "It was just plain weird knowing that he was, like, in the machine. Sam got to be my hero again. I was too confused to know what to do. Anyway, that's the story."

Lillian just shook her head. "Families. What goes around really does come around, doesn't it?"

By afternoon, they'd turned the store over to Jamie, having decided that a bracing walk on the beach would be a good idea.

It wasn't.

The air was so cold that their teeth were chattering under the mufflers wrapped around their mouths and their foreheads hurt.

"Let's g-go someplace w-warm," Charlie said. "If the air gets any f-fresher, we'll freeze."

Lillian nodded numbly and they trudged off the windswept sand of the beach and eventually into a tavern with a view of it. They unwrapped themselves like mummies, feeling just about that dry, and ordered two foamy glasses of stout and hot appetizers. Then two more glasses of stout.

"Delicious," Lillian said, licking foam from her upper lip. "But so filling."

"Mmm. It's nice in here," Charlie replied. "So cozy."

The afternoon light cast lengthening shadows

as the winter day drew to a close. They had no idea of how long they'd been there, feeling too well-fed and a bit buzzed. The conversation begun in the bookstore had continued, and Lillian seemed to be growing a tad sentimental on the subject of families.

To be expected, Charlie thought, sipping her second stout. Lillian didn't really seem to have one. Daydreaming, she sensed the older woman was studying her and looked up. Yikes. Lillian had tears in her eyes.

"Can I tell you something, Charlie?" she asked softly.

Double yikes. What could it be? Charlie couldn't very well say no. "Sure," she answered.

"When you moved in next door, it felt—it felt like a circle had closed. You know I knew your father, of course."

Charlie nodded. It seemed to be true confessions time. A couple of drinks, a couple of women in a secluded booth—it happened.

"Well . . ." Lillian took a deep breath, followed by a huge swig of stout. She set the foamy glass down, then picked it up again and drained it. "Here goes nothing."

Charlie propped her chin on her hand. Whatever Lillian was going to say, it might take her a while to find the words. All she, Charlie, could do was wait.

"He hadn't married your mother yet when he met a friend of mine. A flower child. A free spirit. And he got her pregnant."

Charlie sat up very straight. Her hands dropped into her lap and twisted. Lillian was getting straight to the point.

"She called herself Astral Moony, but no one knew what her real name was. Anyway, she had the baby and took off. No one ever heard from her again."

"Was I that baby?" Charlie asked, her voice strangled.

Lillian nodded. "But I took care of you. Until your father met your mother. So your father is your father and your mother is your mother, because she raised you and loved you and Astral didn't."

Charlie was speechless. It was hard to imagine her conservative father, who was pure Prescott, consorting with a flower child. But she trusted Lillian, who had no reason to lie to her.

"I was waiting for the right time to tell you. I'm sorry," Lillian said. "It's a bombshell, I know. But there you go. You were literally left on my doorstep."

"Was I a good baby?"

"An angel." Lillian began to sniffle. "Never a minute of trouble. I didn't want to give you up, but you weren't mine."

"I was for a little while."

"Not long."

"Did anyone else in Edgartown know?"

Lillian shook her head. "Astral had you at a mainland hospital and brought you back here. She was, you know, kind of a flake, so no one asked many questions. Sometimes being really different is the same as being invisible. People didn't want to know, put it that way. But I never thought it was a good idea not to tell you."

"I'm glad you did," Charlie said sincerely. "But wow. That's a lot to take in." She sat back, completely amazed.

"Your dad, Michael, was thinking about telling you and then he died unexpectedly. Your mom never did decide."

"So that left you."

Lillian bit back a sob. "Yes. And when you and I started going through the archives and really talking about family, and it seemed to make you so sad, all I could think was . . . no more lies. Ghosts shouldn't have that kind of power over the living but they do, sometimes."

"I found that out," Charlie said wryly.

"Anyway, dear, the past and the present can't be separated."

"I remember you saying that," Charlie murmured. "I understand." She thought for a while in silence. Actually, Lillian's revelation was going to help her understand a lot of things.

"There's one more thing," Lillian said. "You must be wondering why I told you now. It's almost Christmas and the holidays are hard enough. Why didn't I wait?" she asked rhetorically.

"I don't mind," Charlie reassured her.

Lillian gave her a wistful look. "This was going to be your first Christmas on your own. And I didn't want you to think that you didn't have family. I mean, you don't. People pass away and run away and those ties break, whether we want them to or not. But . . ." she hesitated. "You still do have me, Charlie. For always. Think of me as your fairy bookmother or something. Or your once-upon-a-time aunty. Can you do that?"

Charlie pressed her lips together, feeling tears well in her own eyes. "Yes," she whispered. "I think so. Thank you, Lillian. For the brownies and cookies and the good advice and friendship. And for everything that I never knew you did for me, most of all."

It was another hour before they left and went their separate ways. Charlie bundled up again and wandered around town, thinking and thinking and thinking. Tired out, she called Sam on her cell from the doorway of a store that had shuttered for the season and asked him to meet her in town. Between the two stouts and Lillian's astonishing revelation, she was feeling a little unsteady.

He heard it in her voice. "You okay, Charlie? Did something happen?"

"I—ah—may have sprained something. I'm not sure."

"What? Where does it hurt?"

My heart. My soul. What she told him was a complete lie. "My foot."

She felt a surge of happiness when she saw his familiar, broad-shouldered body leaning into the stiff wind to come and get her. His hands were jammed in his pockets and the material of the big parka billowed back against his muscular frame.

He looked stalwart. He looked strong enough to carry her all the way home. And that was what he did, not listening to her protests.

They were in front of her house and she could see the Christmas tree through the window. The rest of the lights in the living room had been turned off. But the tree wasn't quite the same. He'd added something. Sam caught her look and asked, "Notice anything new?"

"The star," she said happily. "It's gorgeous. Did you buy that?"

"Yup. It's a top-of-the-line Twinklerama, no less. I know it's only going to be up for another week but I was going to splurge on it anyway. Then the guy at the hardware store gave it to me for half off because I bought so much fix-it stuff. This house needs work. And you need a rest." He adjusted her position in his arms. "And you're going to loll around while I slave and elevate that foot and keep an ice pack on it until I say you can take it off."

She wasn't really listening, just looking at the tree, then at his rugged face, framed by the hood. "That actually sounds romantic. Like we're a couple." She could fake a sprain for an evening, no problem. Eventually she would tell him what Lillian said. They had time.

He hoisted her higher and said indignantly, "Yeah, we are. That's why I came back like I said

I would. That's why I came to get you. That's why I'm going to fix up this place."

"Then what?" she murmured, clinging to him as he managed the latch with one hand without setting her down. He used the toe of his boot to nudge the front door completely open.

"That's why I'm carrying you over the threshold. Practice run," he added quickly. "But I think this you-and-me thing is going to work out fine."

She got the front of his shirt good and wet with happy tears as he took a huge step and just stood there in the entryway, still holding her. "What's the matter?" he asked. "Does that foot hurt?"

"No," she said honestly. "Not at all. Put me on the sofa. Let's take it from there."

The light of the Twinklerama was all they needed.

THE MULLED WINE THAT CHARLIE NEVER GOT TO MAKE

1 bottle of red wine (a fruity merlot or full-bodied
   cabernet works well)
½ cup brandy
½ cup sugar
1 cinnamon stick
6 or 7 whole cloves
orange zest

In a large saucepan over low heat, dissolve the
sugar into the brandy, then add wine and spices.
Heat gently until steaming for about two minutes
and pour into warm mugs.

Orange zest is simply very narrow, very short
slices of orange peel. You can buy dried zest in a
jar in the spice section but to make it yourself, use
a vegetable peeler to take fine shreds from the
peel of a fresh orange. Avoid the white material
(this is called the pith) inside the peel because of
its bitterness. Use only the peel, which is rich in
aromatic oil. And you don't need much—a few
tablespoons of fresh orange zest are enough for
the whole saucepan. Serves three or four.

WICKED GOOD EGGNOG

2 cups whole milk
½ cup dark rum
¼ cup sugar
¼ teaspoon cinnamon
¼ teaspoon nutmeg
½ cup whipped cream or more, to taste

In a mixing bowl, dissolve the sugar and spices into a little of the rum and beat well. (The alcohol will bring out the flavor of the spices.) Add the rest of the rum. Add the milk. Then add whipped cream to taste, fresh or canned, and fold gently into the milk mixture to give the eggnog body and pour into big glasses or mugs. Serves two.

Nutmeg is what makes eggnog taste like eggnog. As for the characteristic golden color, that used to come from raw egg yolks beaten into milk, with whites whipped to a froth added at the last minute. Not recommended these days! You could froth up packaged, pasteurized egg whites from the dairy case, but they're still sort of icky, though safe. Standard supermarket eggnogs use food coloring, gums, and high-fructose corn sweeteners for that gooey thickness.

CHRISTMAS ZOMBIE

2 oz dark rum
2 oz light rum
½ oz apricot brandy
1 oz fresh lemon juice
1 oz orange juice
1 oz pineapple juice
1 teaspoon sugar
1 cinnamon-candy stick
crushed ice

Fill a cocktail shaker with crushed ice and add dark and light rum, apricot brandy, sugar, and juices. If you don't have one of those glorious gizmos, use a really big glass topped with a double layer of snugly fitted plastic wrap that you hold in place as you shake. Either way, shake well. Pour into tall glasses and garnish with cinnamon-candy stick.

Fresh lemon juice tastes a lot better than the bottled stuff. Roll a fresh lemon firmly under your hand on the kitchen counter to get it juicy inside, slice in two and squeeze, straining out the seeds before you add the juice. Serves one or two (this is strong enough to share, for sure).

GIN AND TONIC

2 oz gin
½ cup tonic (about half of a single-serve bottle)
one fat, juicy fresh lime, cut in quarters
chunky ice

This is a simple drink that gets its refreshing snap from being served very cold. Which means all ingredients should be very cold before you start, including the lime! Cut it in quarters and reserve one for garnish. Squeeze the others, strain seeds. Throw several chunks of ice in chilled glass, then add fresh lime juice. Pour in gin. Add tonic. Garnish with remaining lime wedge. Serves one.